Willem's GOD

Willem's GOD

LINDA STEWART GREEAR

ILLUSTRATED BY BRITTANY SCRUGGS

DEDICATION

For William and Virginia, my good parents;

And to my other grandchildren: Jose, Brian, Nehemiah James, and another on the way!

CONTENTS

ACKNOWLEDGMENTS

THANKS to Lanee Grace Turner, my granddaughter: for working with me on Willem's God all the way through the writing of it, and for even writing a sentence or two.

To Bill Turner, my grandson: for proof-reading and, most of all, for being the inspiring model for Willem.

To Lee Turner, my daughter: for helping me publish Willem's God: without whose expertise and willingness to assist me, it could not have happened.

To friends, Ms. Melissa Causey, Bartow Public Library Youth Services Librarian; Brother George Henson; and my sister, Barbara Stewart: for valuable suggestions and encouragement.

To Brother Gene Toth: for artistically preparing Willem's God for publishing.

And thanks always to Michael Greear, my husband: All much.

FOREWORD

ONE of the models for Willem was my grandson, Bill Turner. He helped me edit the book, and often recognized himself in it. Also Willem is much like the other model, Bill's great-grandfather, William E. (Bill) Stewart.

My daddy Bill Stewart was counted a "King of the Kids" when he was a boy. He was raised in Reading, Pennsylvania. The story we knew about him was he ran away as a teenager and hoboed trains to Florida in the late 1930's. He was searching for his mother's daddy, thought to be living in Arcadia, Florida. Also he was following his brother Reid, who had come to Florida earlier to look for their grandfather.

It's a mystery to me how long it took Daddy to get all the way to the southern State and what he did along the way. When the freckled young man finally arrived in Arcadia in southwest Florida, he learned his grandfather was dead, and Reid had found work and lodging at the Brantley farm north of Arcadia. Reid had married Elon, one of the Brantley girls. Later, Bill married her sister Virginia, my mother.

He lived near there for the rest of his life, because he loved the creeks and wild fields of rural Florida. Daddy fished the branches and rode his stud-horse Rocket over the untamed pastures, working as a cowboy for the local cattlemen.

He bought a never-painted cracker house slouching on the corner of twenty acres of land. The old house had two bedrooms and no bathroom, and eventually all seven of us lived in it. He never painted it or built us a bathroom. Not until Mama showed him she could save up enough money to build a new block home, did he agree to leave it.

I visited Reading, PA, for the first time after Daddy died. My husband drove me through a city shaped like a bowl. Inside the bowl I was surprised to discover street after street of narrow 3-story apartments with stoops, swarming with people. "No wonder he ran away," I told Michael as I cried. "My daddy had to escape this!"

Bill Stewart's escape was the model for Willem's dream. But that's where the likeness ends. As far as I know, Daddy didn't yearn to know God in his younger years as Willem does. And then Willem finds a new dream...

If you are a boy reading this, I pray you will meet a friend in Willem. You might discover that like Willem, Jesus Christ knows you, and He loved you first.

Sister Linda

Nobody knows how the

first news of Jesus Christ came to the

imperial city of Rome.

Perhaps it came like this . . .

A.D. 34

PROLOGUE

LANEE'S long silky hair waved behind her as she raced down the dusty road home. She was the first to leave the church this morning. After she whispered to Eema, she'd slipped out the door and hurried onto the hot dirt road.

Oh, my! Brother Thaddaeus really preached the glory down. The Holy Ghost filled the synagogue with the power of Pentecost! It's happening in Arbela! The thrill boosted her speed.

Spotting the old sycamore tree at the front door, she fast-walked up to it then hurried past it into the coolness of their stone house. Up the low stairs, she breezed right on through her room out to the rooftop.

The cool plaster of the parapet surrounding the rooftop felt good against her hot cheek. She whispered, "Jesus?"

Then the pretty fifteen-year-old lifted her head and gazed toward the grassy fields stretching out behind the house. *We met there, Lord.* She remembered His voice...His words...His presence.

Jesus?

Only strong silence answered her.

Lanee raised her imploring hazel eyes toward the clear blue sky. *There is something I need to know, Lord...truly you're helping our neighbors...oh, thank you for that...but remember, you told me to go into all the world and preach to the little ones. When, Lord? How, Lord?*

Lanee jumped when noisy cicadas started up their buzzing

answer. *Saviour, please.* She gripped the plaster wall harder as if it were Jesus' arm. *I must have your answer.*

The buzzing subsided and died out. Closing her eyes, she began softly reciting the Psalm she'd studied with Savta, "I waited patiently for the LORD, and he inclined unto me and heard my cry..."

Ever so naturally the boy's face appeared behind her closed lids.

Oh, my... She held still, fearing the vision would disappear as quickly as it came. The boy's image was so distinct that Lanee could even see the freckles sprinkled over his round face. She wondered at his troubled expression.

As she stared, a strong wind sprang up in the vision. It moved through his hair and molded his tunic against his stout frame. Then Lanee saw his face light up with gladness for the wind.

"Who is he, Lord?" she asked.

The answer came, clearly, lovingly: *Willem.*

CHAPTER ONE

THE GREAT SEA

I CUPPED my hands around my mouth, "Hello to the Bella! Ju-li-an! We've come to help you unload!"

Only a moment elapsed before his rough bass voice yelled back, "Never mind, you scamp! You boys go on back to the city—I'll unload this myself!"

I waited for the boat to drift closer. "We'll help you for free," I answered. "You don't have to even give us a pear!"

As soon as he threw the rope out, Senny grabbed it and tied it to the pier. Then we all skittered aboard and started lifting heavy baskets of lemons.

Julian grabbed my arm. "Ok, Willem, what's the reason for all this gratis help?"

I squinted at his leathery face trying to size up my chance of success. Giving him my best smile, I said, "We want to go back down the river with you. We'd like to sail to the Great Sea."

11

I kept smiling when behind him I saw the surprise start up on my frats' faces. I heard Blue's soft whistle, and Leo gave me a thumbs up sign.

Julian let go of my arm and turned his back on me. "No."

I walked around him and stuck my round freckled face right up to Julian's nose. "We'll find our own way back—let us go with you this one time. You don't have to feed us. We can all swim. We'll even help you clean the boat before we leave today."

Julian stared back at me and said his final word. "Mothers."

I thought a minute. "You leave early; we'll return before they miss us."

I saw the master of the boat's frozen resolve thaw just a little. *Maybe!* I grabbed a basket of grapes, hefted it up to the dock, and went back for more.

We worked with Julian for a long hour unloading the crowded ship's deck. Customers began gathering around the piles of fresh fruit, and soon Julian's whole attention was on haggling over the sales.

Blue passed me carrying a heavy crate of oranges, as I hurried to pull another one off the stack. "Think he'll take us, Willem?"

I just grunted out loud as I pulled the full basket off the top.

Senny and I lifted the last baskets onto the dock while the rest got busy emptying buckets of river water over the deck and sweeping it off.

Dripping sweat and glad to be through, we joined Julian on the dock. All he had left were a few baskets of apples. We glanced at each other, waiting, as he stood counting his money.

"What time, Julian?" I asked.

The ship's captain looked up at me and over at the wet deck of the Bella. He scratched at his neck with the hand full of coins. Then he sighed and said, "At first light."

~~~

"Willem."

Uh-oh.

"Yes, Mater."

"I'm going down to the shop now. I left you some porridge. Sleep awhile, then come down and help me some today."

Not today!

"M-Mater?"

"What?"

"I need to do something else, today."

"Since when do you choose?"

"Mater, may I help you tomorrow instead?"

"What are you into, Willem?"

If I tell her she'll NEVER let me go.

"I...I can't tell you. But I promise I'll be back before dark."

Then she stood over my cot. "Willem, I don't want to fuss with you. If you won't tell me what you're doing, you can't go. You'll stay in the shop with me all day!"

There's no other way. "M-Mater...I won't! I mean, this is too important to me. I can't obey you this time!"

"Willem!" We stared at each other.

Oh, no! Mater's eyes were filling up with tears.

Then she started. "What can I do? I could lash you, and forbid you—still you will go. I could get you up and make you

13

go to the shop right now, but as soon as my back is turned, you will go. I am too tired to fight you. But remember as you go, I am unhappy with you, my only son. Remember."

Then she left.

Worse than ever!

I got up and dressed. *Oh, Mater!* Weighed down low, I ate the porridge she'd left me. Still, I slipped out the door, down the two flights of stairs, and out into the street.

It's only this one time I'll get to see the Great Sea—I can't stay home today.

After a few more steps, I shrugged, trying to get loose from the sadness…and guilt.

But, I'm going to dip my foot in the Great Sea today!

By the time I went around the back to dodge the front of Mater's shop, I felt the sadness changing into excitement— *Mater will be all right. She always is.*

The sun wasn't up yet. I checked around the corner before I turned it. Thieves sometimes lurked nearby. The shop wasn't in the safest part of town. I didn't see anyone, so I hurried on around the insula, our three-story apartment building.

The street was empty except for a few dogs and other early shopkeepers opening their stalls. Leo, always light on his feet, slipped up behind me with, "Bo!" for a greeting. It scared me but I tried not to show it.

I gave short shrill whistles, and out came the twins, Turk and Blue. Big Senny, stretching wide to wake up, was waiting for us on his stoop. He finished tying the strap of his sandal as he whispered to me, "I didn't tell Mater I'm going. You sure we'll be back before dark?"

I hope so, I thought, but I said, "Sure we will."

The slap of our sandals and a rooster crowing disturbed the only quiet time there was in Rome for the day. We hurried across the city to the Tiber.

Me and my frats will leave you for the first time, Big Dirty, and you won't even know we're gone! Today I'm going away from you, Ugly Rome, to step into the clean water of the Great Sea!

At the pier, we saw Julian looking in our direction. He was ready to cast off. We ran up to him, grinning, and got on board.

The boat slipped down the river through the dozing city. A stiff morning breeze filled up the triangular sail as the sun came up. It burned the sides of our faces as we traveled south through Rome.

Julian motioned to us, "There's the imperial palace!" And we all ran to lean over the rail and look into the blazing sun. Shielding our eyes, we could see flags flying and the praetorian guards everywhere, looking tiny in the distance.

Soon the city and the sun were behind us as we sailed on to Ostia. I sucked in the fresh air that blew over my face—the first *fresh* air I'd ever breathed. How good it was!

"Look!" Turk cried out. Fine houses, with green lawns running almost down to the river bank, appeared. I'd never seen such homes.

We passed other loaded-down corbitas pulled by slaves toward Rome. *Maybe we can get a ride back on one.* I felt another twinge of guilt, for I didn't know how we'd make it home to Mater before dark. There was Senny's mother, too.

The breeze became a wind, and soon the fat lazy Bella, mostly empty, flew over the water. We shouted to each other, and I saw Julian's brown face split into a wide grin. When the way was clear, he steered the vessel in a zig-zag path to make us cry out louder.

Soon the high apartment buildings of Ostia could be seen. They were much like the insulas we lived in—arched windows on second and third stories with shops underneath. Julian pointed out a huge building right beside the river, "Filled to the top with grain from all over the world," he said, laughing, "to feed all of you Roman's hungry mouths!"

When he steered the boat around the next bend, suddenly there it was—the Great Sea! I looked, then closed my eyes, and opened them again. It was real!

Julian yelled, "All right boys—you said you can swim—jump out!"

And that's just what we did. Leo's foot touched the rail and he launched himself. I wasn't so quick, and when I hit the water I was shocked by how cold it was and then doubly shocked to taste the salt in it. I swam for shore and spat, crawling out at last onto the sandy beach.

I heard my frats' loud whooping, and suddenly Turk and Blue got hold of me and pulled me up to see what they'd discovered—piles of amazing seashells—stars, swirls, fans, flat discs, tiny butterflies.

Senny with his hands full cried out, "I'm taking some of these home to Mater!"

I felt my heart take a leap! *I knew it would be here— something unbelievable!* I ran up to the shell pile and picked up a beautiful swirl of a shell. I bent over it and studied the amazing thing. It spiraled out with little rooms built bigger and bigger as it swirled. I'd never seen anything like it.

We made tall piles of the beautiful shells beside a palm tree. "How are we going to get them home, Willem?" Leo asked.

How will I explain them to Mater?

I just shrugged then struck out up the beach toward the town. "Food's this way!"

Later we strolled back toward the beach munching on barley bread spread with bean paste. The money bag hanging from my waist was flatter, but our stomachs were feeling much better.

We took a turn behind one of the grain silos and discovered a large burlap bag with a hole in the bottom. Senny tied up the bottom, and slung it around his neck—it would do just fine to carry our shells.

It didn't take us long to discover the fun of catching waves and riding them back into shore. The bigger they got, the louder we laughed. And the hours flew by. I noticed the sun was getting low as I stretched out to rest on the sand.

That's when I felt worry creep into my mind.

I argued with it. *Maybe Simeon will come today. Yes, Simeon would take us home.* I hadn't seen my Jewish friend, Rabbi Saul's son, for many weeks. He brought goods for their shop from everywhere...*if he would just show up today.*

Lying on my stomach with my head on my arms, I closed my eyes and remembered the rabbi's overflowing store. Just around the corner and down a ways from Mater's cheese shop, it was always filled with Hebrew-gabbling customers. Old Rabbi Saul never chased anyone out, even if they didn't buy a *tack.*

I'm not quite sure when I began to understand what they were saying. It just began to make sense to me one day while I sat on my favorite spot by the sandal display. From then on the store was much more interesting. I especially liked to hear the rabbi's comments to the women who shopped there.

"Oh, so you're going to be giving your daughter a party? Is she the same little girl who chews on her braids and crosses her eyes at me? Better wait until she *deserves* that party."

"No, Rabbi, my little Elise would never do such things. She is the best girl in our insula."

Yes, the rabbi had told the truth, for Elise was worse than he said. The rabbi peered into the mother's eyes, nudging her with his wisdom then smiled when he said, "You are her eema. You should know."

I really laughed at that.

A seagull's raspy call pulled me back to the sandy beach. I suddenly realized how late it was! Jumping up, I whistled and yelled, "Let's get back to the harbor. It's time to go home!"

My fraters shook off the water as they ran. Senny grabbed the bag stashed behind the palm tree, and we all trudged to the pier where the Tiber ran into the Great Sea. The pier felt hot under our sand-crusted feet. At the pier's end, we sat down, brushed off the sand, and tied on our damp sandals.

Turk asked, "What's the plan for getting home, Willem?" His eyes were red from the salt water.

I searched the barges being harnessed to the slave gangs. I didn't recognize any of the captains, so I said, "Let's get a snack in town."

We all gobbled down a handful of raisins and a boiled egg each. Too tired to talk, we trudged back to the pier. We sat down and swung our feet over the water, watching the sun sink into the sea. When it was half gone, I got really worried and was about to tell my frats we'd have to spend the night there. But, squinting into the sunset, I saw the silhouette of another fat corbita sailing into the mouth of the Tiber.

We watched it dock instead of hooking up to be pulled. They must have something to unload in Ostia. The captain came ashore. He was dressed in a long tunic and had a full beard.

Startling my frats, I cried out with pure relief, "Perfectus!"

Then I jumped up and yelled, "Simeon! It's me—Chezek!"

CHAPTER TWO

I HAVE A PATER!

I CARRIED my sandals up the squeaking outside stairs and pushed open the door. *So tired!* The noise of the night wagons pulling freight into Rome became muffled as soon as I pulled the door to. As I crept to my cot, I saw the curtain around Mater's was open. I made out her form lying still. I listened.

Yes! Her breathing is steady! Perfectus duplus! Quietly placing the sandals beside my cot, I pulled the covers back, and crawled in. As I relaxed, I closed my eyes and saw it again. As far as the eye could see rhythmic tossing waves of blue-green water, sand underfoot, shells just lying around for the taking, boats from everywhere in the world, seabirds crying—*and me and my frats in the middle of it all!*

Then for some reason I opened my eyes. The lightened windows revealed Mater staring down at me through the dark veil of her loose hair. Her eyes looked swollen, and oh, so angry!

"M-Mater, I'm home," I offered. My stomach went into knots.

"Yes, son, I can see that. Where have you been all day and all night?"

"I-I don't think you want to know."

"Yes, son, I do want to know. In fact I WILL KNOW or you will not be able to rise from this cot tomorrow after I get through with your backside!"

"I-I went to see...the Great Sea!" It started out as a confession. But then it changed. "Oh, Mater, you should see it! The gulls, the boats, the waves..." My voice trailed off when I saw the shock on Mater's face in the moonlight.

"You...You are not yet...twelve years old! How did you get to the Great Sea?"

"A friend of mine has a boat."

"Who is this *friend?*"

"You don't know him."

"Willem, I'm more upset than you've ever known me to be tonight! Can you see that?"

"Yes, Mater."

"Tonight, lying here in the midst of Rome, this wicked city, I have imagined you abused and killed in a hundred different ways. I had given you up only five minutes before you came sneaking in."

"I-I'm sorry."

"Tomorrow you will help me in the shop, and the next day and the next. You will go nowhere without my permission. You are too young to be on your own!"

I was scared, but still I wanted to cry out, *Mater, I can't be tied down!*

But not tonight—she was too upset to argue with.

"I wish I had never come to this horrible city," she moaned. Then in a quieter voice she added "...but then, I wouldn't have you."

Tired and scared as I was, I listened hard for what she'd say next. I'd wondered so often. *Do I have a pater? Do we have any other family anywhere?*

"What do you mean?" I squeaked out.

She walked over to the window, and looked out across the pavement toward the next row of apartments. Then she surprised me when she came back, knelt down, and took my hand.

"Son, I need to tell you something."

Whatever she was going to tell me didn't matter right then as much as hearing the hard anger gone from her voice. "What is it, Mater?"

She moved closer and lowered her eyes toward mine. "Tonight while I was so worried about you, I thought if I ever saw you again, I would tell you about your pater."

A streak of excitement ran through me. "My pater?"

"Yes, Willem. Your pater is a soldier. He is gone…actually he has been posted in Gaul for most of your life. We were not allowed to marry, because no Roman soldier can. Many living around here are also soldiers' families."

I have a pater! Then I couldn't help it—big tears jumped up in my eyes. They spilled over and ran down the sides of my face. I felt them rolling through my hair. I was glad Mater wasn't looking down at me right then.

"I have the shop which he bought for me. He sends me money to support the shop and you. He knows about you and has seen you when you were very small. His name is Lucius Dio."

I couldn't believe my ears. I had wondered so long why I never had a father, though neither Senny nor Turk and Blue ever had a man living with them since they'd lived near me. *My pater is a soldier, a Roman soldier!*

Then I sobbed out, "Oh, Mater, thank you for telling me.

And forgive me for scaring you today! I will try never to do it again."

Suddenly I sat up, realizing I had made a promise I couldn't keep.

"Please try to understand me, Mater. I must see—I must know—I must be allowed to explore. Please allow me to! I can't live shut up in the box of the shop!"

Sighing, she put her arms around me. "Don't you know I do understand you? Yet, what is best for you? You are a child, and I can't let you do as you please yet." She kissed the top of my head.

I hoped that meant she wouldn't remember about making me work in the shop.

"So, Willem, as I said, you will help me in the shop tomorrow and all the rest of the week." She got up and went to her cot. "I need to go to bed now. I am very tired. Good night, son."

~~~

Cheese! Surrounded by every kind, with every smell, from every sort of cow, sheep, or goat that could produce milk! Some smelled so strong we had to hide it, only bringing it out when a customer asked for it. We sold cheeses with red rinds, black rinds, and some in little cloth bags hanging from the rafters of the shop.

It's a good thing I like cheese.

I cleaned the counter with an old rag.

The first day of my prison sentence...I wonder what Senny is doing. Did his mater take it as badly as mine did?

It seemed like five or six hours went hobbling by before a customer came through the door. But instantly I was interested, for it was a soldier! *Could this be my pater?* He was portly and when he removed his helmet I saw he had red hair. *Probably not.*

"Sir! May I help you find a cheese you would like?" I inspected his tunic and jingling army belts as he sniffed and peered around.

"I'd like to taste this one."

"Yes sir!"

I sliced off a piece of the cheese with a sharp knife and handed it to him. After just a taste, he bought the whole cheese, and I put the money in the till. As he turned toward the door, I said, "Sir, may I ask you a question?"

"What is it, boy?"

"Have you ever been to Gaul?"

"Why do you ask?"

"I-I would like to know what it's like there."

"Yes. I've been there. Lived there for two years."

"Did you ever know a soldier there named Lucius Dio?"

The soldier stared at me with hard eyes. He stopped chewing on the cheese, and peered more closely at me. "No, I've never heard that name. Sorry, son."

I watched him leave thinking he'd lied to me. Suddenly I realized why—he wouldn't want to get involved in the problem of a soldier having a child.

I shouldn't have asked him.

Mater came up front and said, "Did you make a sale?"

"Yes, a man bought a whole cheese." I didn't want to tell her the man was a soldier. Nor that I had asked about Pater.

"Oh, good. What kind? I'll bring one from the back."

My three days in prison finally were spent. Mater had done every chore she could think of while I tended the store. The last day all I had my mind on was getting loose— *I'll go, go, GO—somewhere, anywhere, away from this shop full of cheese!*

"All right, Willem, you've been a great help to me. I'm releasing you from being storekeeper and promoting you to delivery boy. But you must promise not to make any secret trips out of Rome, if I let you go."

My answer was a dash for the back room, pulling off my dirty apron as I ran. She laughed.

"First, son, take a trip to the bath," she said. "When you get back I'll have your package ready."

The delivery I had to make was the stinkiest cheese we sold. *I should have taken my bath after this delivery!* I poked it into my back sack, and began the trek across town toward the Via Sacra. *One day, I'll take a boat down the Tiber and never come back!* I dodged the other people using the pavement. I saw them turn to see where the rank smell was coming from.

My thoughts came in rhythm with my steps down the pavement. *I'll find me a place to live away from all these people and buildings. I'll camp by the water until I can build me a house. I'll raise my own food—chickens, pigs, a cow—I'll have a dog and a cat! I'll bring all my friends along, and when we get everything set up we'll send for our mothers.*

Just then I had to cross the street to avoid a pile of garbage rotting outside a tall apartment building. *I'll dig a big hole a long way behind my house to throw my garbage in.*

I crossed back again to avoid the entrance to the public bath. *I'll have my own private bath and toilet, and I'll keep it clean.*

Suddenly I realized these were my dreams before I knew I had a pater. What would he think of my dreams? Would he want to come live with me? Would he want to live with all of my friends? Maybe he'd not let me buy the land or move away. That alarmed me. *I can't live here forever—I'll die!*

It could have been the smell of the cheese drifting up the back of my neck that made Rome seem so ugly today, so I hurried. Finally I turned onto the street that led to the marble temple of the Vestal Virgins. *I'll not build any temples when I leave Rome!* I went around to the back of the building, and knocked at the wooden door.

"Willem! Enter, my friend." It was Draco, a bigger man than anyone I'd ever known, and he was a slave. "So it is you I smelled. Here, unload that sack before it becomes a permanent attribute."

Draco always spoke Greek to me.

"Who can eat this, Draco?" I replied in Greek.

"Oh, it is *Her Highness,* Octavia. She is so unhappy that

her cheese must be potent, her wine must be syrup, and her friends must know all the latest gossip to distract her."

"Why?"

"She has fallen in love with one of her slaves. He has no love for her, and also knows it is forbidden. She's not allowed to marry until her stint as a Vestal Virgin is over. That's years from now. Here's your money, boy. Come back to see me another day and we will play darts again."

I thought about Octavia as I retraced my steps away from the Forum area to our insula. I had seen her once. She had stood at the inner kitchen door when I'd brought some cheese. About Mater's age, but not as pretty. Her hair looked dirty and matted. Her sad eyes raked me over once, and she turned away. *I'll not have any slaves in my new land. And maybe I'll invite Octavia to come and enjoy my place.*

Though I knew I couldn't live in this crowded city for many more years, every thought of Pater seemed to drown out the joy I once found in my dreams. Oh, who is he? And why don't I even know what he would think of my plans?

Suddenly a new idea hit me—*maybe we can make some money by selling the shells we found at the Great Sea. If I had enough money to buy the land, my pater would know I mean business about leaving.* The two wrestling worries calmed down inside me.

After I handed the cheese money over to Mater, I gathered up my fraters and said, "We're going to try to sell our shells in the Forum tomorrow. I'll whistle for you early."

So, we all got to the Forum as the sun came up and grabbed an empty spot. Senny spread an old blanket on the pavement where we displayed all the sandy shells we'd found at the Great Sea. I tried to arrange our goods as nicely as I'd seen Rabbi Saul display his.

Blue nodded at the hinged clam-shell, "I think that'll be the first to sell. It's sweet!"

"If it weren't for this starfish I found, that might be true!" Leo said.

This rough brown shell I had found was my favorite. I passed my thumb over the utter smoothness on the inside, and wondered how much I could ask for it. That was something I hadn't thought of. *Mater always sets the price for her cheeses. How?*

I decided to ask my first customer to make an offer. She was a young matron followed by her slave girl who was carrying a large empty basket. She inquired, "Will you take a sesterce for that one that is like a star?"

I boldly answered, "That's much too low a price for such a beautiful shell brought all the way from the Great Sea. Surely you know what it's really worth."

The woman looked at me, and I squinted back at her. I hoped she could see that I knew what I was talking about. And surely my expression must have been just right, for she offered me more for it than I'd dreamed of asking. When she left, the boys all whooped over the sale.

So I handled the customers from then on. Meanwhile Turk and Blue shopped for breakfast, and Leo and Senny just nosed around the rest of the market. The hinged clam shell went next—close to how Blue predicted. Then someone wanted the very one I hated to part with. It was a well-dressed elderly man who was suddenly there peering into my hand. I had been day-dreaming as I caressed the smooth beautiful interior of the shell.

He coughed into the sleeve of his pallium then whispered, "How much for that one, boy?" He coughed again.

"Er...I'd like ten denarii for this one, sir," I surprised myself by saying.

"Do you know what it is called, son?" he said in a little stronger voice. He straightened up and studied me.

"No sir, I only know it is beautiful."

"It is called an abalone, and I have not seen a more beautiful one. The smooth interior is called mother of pearl. Excuse me a moment." He bent over at the waist to cough several times. Then he looked up and said, "Where did you get it?"

"I found it near Ostia on the beach of the Great Sea."

"I will take it and any others that you may find. Here's your money. If you find any more like it, bring them to me, and I will give you the same amount for them." The long speech caused him another coughing spell.

I handed it over, amazed that he had paid so much. "Surely, sir. Where can I find you?"

"The Praetorian Camp. Ask for Nicholas. I am the steward there. What's *your* name?"

"Willem," I said and smiled, even though I missed the smooth silky feel of my special shell.

As he left I thought, *The steward of the soldiers' camp! Maybe he knows something about Lucius Dio. He is very old. Could it be that he knew my pater before he was sent to Gaul?*

That thought chased around in my mind as I sold more and more of the shells. The blanket was soon empty, even of all the little butterflies, and we had our little bag full of money! I hid the bag down the front of my tunic, and we gathered up our display blanket and hurried through the streets toward home.

The feeling of that money bag lying against my chest caused me to tell my fraters that I planned to leave Rome. "I need some space. I need to be able to have a whole house to live in, and I want to have animals. I'd like to try to grow things. I'd like to hunt and fish."

"Willem, you're not going without us?" Turk and Blue both cried out at the same time.

I was always surprised when they did that. But they *were* twins. You sure couldn't tell from looking at them—Turk had straight blond hair and brown eyes, and Blue had red frizzy hair and bright blue eyes.

Senny said, "You know that's never going to happen!"

"Of course there's room in my plan for you," I said. "I was hoping you would all want to come."

"When can we go and find us a place, Bo?"

"Not yet, Leo. It's going to cost money. That's why I wanted to sell the shells today. Would you all like to pool our money together until we get enough?"

They agreed. Then Senny asked, "What will we do with the money now, Willem? We need much more, and we need a place to keep it as we save."

I already had an idea, so I said, "I will ask Rabbi Saul. He will know. Until then, Senny, ask your mother to hold it for us." Mater Sophia was a woman who could be trusted. She would guard it with her life. I looked around to make sure no one was watching, then handed him the bag.

When we reached our insula, we split up, and I stepped

into the cheese shop before I went upstairs. I needed to talk something over with Mater. Soon we must make another trip to the Great Sea!

CHAPTER THREE

THE BARGAIN

MATER surprised me. I told her about the shells and she got really excited. She wants to go with me to get more—says she wants to meet Julian and pay him for taking us. After that, (if he passes inspection) she's going to talk to my friends' maters about letting them go!

I turned into the rabbi's store still feeling surprised at her. "Chezek!"

"Shalom, Rabbi Saul." I carried our full money bag. "May I talk to you? Can you spare a minute?"

"Oh, sounds like important business! I will finish painting this sign then I'll be with you. Sit—don't you see your spot is empty?—sit!"

I did, and for the thousandth time looked Rabbi's jam-packed store over. I scanned the tools section in the back—it looked like he'd sold a large shovel and one of the hammers that lined the back wall. The paving stones and lumber were piled up even higher in the back corner than I remembered. Simeon must have restocked. The other back corner was spilling out with burlap bags of grain and beans.

Then I sniffed at the special display around the front counter. Tiny perfume jars sent their nose-tingling fragrances out to mingle with all the others—pepper, tanned leather, and the best-worse smelling of all foods, a jug of liquamen, my favorite Roman sauce. How could rotten fish taste so good? I could smell the bread baked in various shapes,

33

sprinkled with black seeds or smooth and polished. It was piled high, threatening to topple down to the concrete floor, or onto the baskets of brown and speckled eggs nearby.

My favorite area in Rabbi's store was right beside his money box on the counter—low barrels of baked sweets and smoked fish, a clay jar of pickled eggs, a pile of shiny lemons, and a mound of tempting red grapes.

Then in the middle of the store were the sheets and towels, scissors and pins, sandals, togas, aprons, knives and swords, mirrors and combs, dishes and pots, harnesses and girdles, styluses and writing tablets. One day I decided to really explore the place and discovered some of the old stuff had been covered over by new stuff. So, Rabbi Saul probably didn't know what all he had for sale.

The rabbi wiped his hands on his soiled apron, and smoothed his long grey beard then picked up the sign. It said, *OPEN LATE EVERY DAY— CLOSED THE SABBATH.*

"How does it look, Chezek?"

I smiled and nodded.

I liked how he called me *Chezek* instead of Willem. He'd been calling me that since I was five years old. That night Mater had taken my hand and we'd walked around the corner and down the next block to Rabbi Saul's store. She was going to buy a new apron. Simeon was at the front door hauling in a wagonload of goods.

I wanted to help, so I let go of Mater's hand and ran to the wagon. I held out my arms for Simeon to give me something to carry. He only gave me a small package of combs. I said, "More!" Simeon piled on another small pack of goods. "More!" I kept on saying the same thing until the pile was above my head. Finally I began to carry it all through the door. Somehow I made it in without dropping anything!

When Rabbi Saul unloaded me, he said, "A fine job, Chezek!" The name stuck, and I've liked it ever since. It's Hebrew for *strong.*

"Now, son, what did you want with me?" Rabbi Saul pulled up an empty barrel and sat down next to me.

I looked him in the eye and said, "If you had some money you wanted to save, what would you do with it?"

Rabbi's merry brown eyes gazed back into mine.

With him looking at me like that, even Rome didn't seem so bad.

"Ay, yes, money to save. I've had money to save in my life. In fact I am saving money now. How, you ask? I bought the boat Simeon sails to bring us more goods for my store. Look around, Chezek, this is how I save my money."

"But, Rabbi, what if there is a fire? What if someone breaks in and steals it all?"

"That's another way I save my money. I bought this whole insula and have been using my money to remodel it with concrete, replacing the flimsy material of which it was first constructed. I have also bought some strong locks for the doors."

"At night, after the store is closed, and you have all the money from the sales, how do you keep it safe?"

"Chezek, you wouldn't be asking me to divulge my secrets to you so you can rob me?" His eyes teased, and I had to smile.

"No, Rabbi. But wherever you put your money, would you be willing to keep mine in that same safe spot?"

"How long will you want me to keep it?"

"Until I can get enough to buy a piece of land outside of Rome."

"Well…it seems my little Chezek has a dream! Very well, son, I will keep your money. Bring it in tonight before I close, and I will put it with my own and keep it safe for you."

As I left the rabbi's store, I thought again of Nicholas, the soldier's steward, and of the beautiful abalone shell I'd found on the beach. *There must be many more lying on the beach for the taking.* I grinned to myself.

Then I noticed how empty the usually crowded streets were. When I heard the roar of the crowd at the Circus Maximus, I knew why.

I'll never go there again.

It's because Mater doesn't want me to go. And… because I disobeyed her once.

The chariot races were the most exciting thing I'd ever seen! But then…the men fought and suddenly one man was down in the dirt begging for mercy, and then…

I'll never go there again.

The crowd roared as I rounded the corner to my insula. Bratty Elise was sitting right in my path. Her braids were all fuzzy, and her big brown eyes were glowing toward me.

"Willem, I've been waiting for you!" she said in a mixture of Hebrew and Greek.

There was no way to avoid her so I said, "Hello, you fuzzy bird. Don't you ever comb your hair?"

"Yes, I do, when I want to! Where have you been? I've been waiting here for *hours.*"

I knew that wasn't true, but instead of arguing I said, "Well, what did you want with me?"

"I heard you're going back to the Great Sea, and I want to go, too!"

"You're joking, right?"

"No! I asked my mater, and of course she said I could go."

"There are no girls going, Elise. And that's how I want to keep it."

"All right. Then I won't tell you what I know that you don't."

"Like what?"

"Oh, that's privileged information…that I *would* be willing to share if you'd let me go with you."

I scowled into the annoying brown eyes, but then decided to ignore the bait. I just walked around her and continued down the street. I was feeling really good about how I'd handled her. *I'll never let Elise, of all girls, go with us!*

"It's about your pa…ter…" she called in a sing-songy voice.

I stopped. I turned around. Then of course I walked back to the fuzzy-headed ten-year-old.

"So," she said squinting up at him, "is it a bargain? If I tell you some *valuable* information about your pater, then you will invite me to accompany you and the boys to Mara Nostrum when you go?"

"Tell me, and then I will decide."

"No."

"How would *you* know anything about my pater?"

"My mater allows me into all her grownup conversations—that's how!"

I took a moment to think. "I'll agree to your bargain on one condition—that my mater allows you to go." *I'm sure she won't!*

"*You* must ask her."

37

I wasn't sure about that, but then I nodded my head.

"Your pater is coming back to Rome. He will live at the Praetorian Camp. He will probably be a guard at the palace soon."

Just then the crowd roared at the Circus.

That was exactly how I felt!

Forgetting all about Elise, I hurried toward home.

"Don't forget—ask her!" she called after me.

I ran into the shop and skidded to a stop in front of the counter. Mater took one look at me and dropped the knife she was using. "What is it?"

I started to say what I'd heard then backed down. *She would have told me if she wanted me to know* was all I could think.

Instead I said, "Uh…Mater, what do you think about taking Elise with us to the Great Sea?"

"Willem, you've been out in the sun too long. Your face is all red. Get yourself some grape juice. Sit down and cool off."

I nodded then hurried away.

She called back to me, "That girl doesn't understand the word *no*. How'd she get you to ask me?"

Uh-oh.

"Mater, this cheese is turning green. Have you noticed it?"

"That's the kind it is. Want to taste it?"

My pater will soon be in Rome. Then I could easily go to see him. I could walk right up to him and say, Hello, my pater, it's your own boy, Willem. The thought sent little shivers up my spine. It also robbed me of any desire for food. My stomach was doing little flops and twists.

I lay down on the cot in the back of the shop. Curling up, I closed my eyes.

"Willem?"

"Yes, Mater," answering the best I could.

She walked back to me, wiping her hands on her apron. "Son, what's wrong?"

I couldn't stop the tears, nor could I keep from wailing, "My pater's coming back to Rome!"

CHAPTER FOUR
WILLEM AND THE GODS

AWAKE hours before daylight, I rolled around on my cot thinking up questions with no answers.

Since Pater cannot be married, once he's back in Rome, what will happen to Mater and me? Will he want to be with us and have to stay away? Or will he want us to stay hidden from his real life?

The thought of seeing Pater kept sending sparks of excitement up the back of my neck. *No...I'm not supposed to even be his son!*

Do I look like him? *What if he doesn't want me?* Will he make me stay in Rome?

He may not even care about seeing me. Could he be arrested because of me?

Suddenly in the middle of all that, I had a new thought that made me sit up in my cot. *Maybe the gods could help me with Pater!* Statues of the gods were everywhere in the city. Usually I laughed when I saw their nakedness. *But who cares if they're naked, if they have power to help me with Pater?* Surely they must be powerful. Why else would so many people believe in them?

I got up, and without telling Mater I hurried out of our poorer section of Rome toward the Forum Romanum. Though it was the same place we'd sold our shells, this morning I saw it in a different light—the great *temples* faced the open Forum. For the first time in my life I was going to have a talk with the gods. Surely they would help me!

As I hurried along, I thought over Mater's attitude toward the gods. *She doesn't ever mention them, but she definitely never laughed at them. And she has frowned at me for laughing at them.* Senny and I always have a good laugh especially when we look at them from behind.

I'd never heard the others laugh. Turk and Blue had their lar and penates, and so did Leo's family. When we first became good frats I asked them what good those household gods were. And they mostly just shrugged and didn't answer. But one day Blue looked real serious and said, "The gods are not to be questioned, Willem. They are too powerful."

I was surprised. When I thought of that it made me hurry even more. Surely Blue knew something I didn't. I tried to decide what I'd say when I got there.

When I turned in to the Forum, there he was—a powerful-looking marble man, sitting there naked like it was entirely normal. On either side of him were two not quite as naked marble women. All of them were sitting on a bench just outside their temple. It seemed they were waiting for me.

"Uh...good morning, sir," I said in a whisper to the man of stone. The sign said he was Jupiter. I looked around. Not many people were in the Forum this early. Jupiter, (the sign said, the Great Ruler of the gods) sat there with his wife Juno, and his daughter Minerva. I moved up closer to their bench and whispered again, "Will you help me?" Then I sat down on the pavement in front of them and waited.

I wanted to say, "You see, my pater is a soldier, but I need him, and he's not supposed to have me and..." But I thought I'd wait until I knew he was listening. I waited some more, and then what seemed an hour later, I got up. Blue must be mistaken. This god is just a marble head!

I explored the temple searching for some sign of life. Besides a few other early-morning visitors, it was all just concrete and marble. I looked up into another statue of Jupiter's marble face. This one was inside the temple and was gigantic. I tried to imagine worshiping him. *Like the graves on the roads—dead.* The wall paintings told of the god's great deeds, and also said, *Jupiter wasn't faithful to Juno. She was angry. Jupiter hatched Minerva full-grown out of his head.* I laughed. Nothing was spoken to me—not even displeasure at my laughter, so I left.

I headed toward another temple. It was a temple built for a real man—Julius Caesar. All of us in Rome knew of him. Before I was born he was our first emperor. A great man! A powerful man!

I wonder if he was as crazy as everyone says our emperor is now. I'd heard that when I was younger, Tiberius had killed his best-loved soldier along with all of his family including the children. *Why should I bow to someone who is insane?* It was all so confusing.

I walked up as close as I could to the pedestal of Caesar's statue, and whispered, "Oh, great Caesar, would you help my pater to love me, and to come home to Mater and me?"

I circled around to the other side of him, studying his determined marble face. "I've heard it was you who didn't want your soldiers to marry and have children, but I need my pater."

Caesar's hard lips were silent.

Discouraged, I went in anyhow, and explored the temple, hoping maybe for a secret key to his help. I saw pictures of Caesar's great deeds. The temple's stones were chiseled with words of his fame. Down in my heart I knew—there was no secret key—Julius Caesar was dead. He couldn't answer any of my questions.

The city was waking up, for suddenly I heard music. A parade was coming. Down the pavement of the Forum proceeded a line of well-dressed men weighed down by a great naked statue of a god. They had their togas pulled up over their heads. Slaves playing a harp, some pipes, and a drum came along behind them brightening up the sleepy Forum. A few ragged children, probably hoping for sweets, ran after them.

Maybe this is what I'm looking for! When they come close, I'll ask them if that god has done something wonderful for them.

As they drew near, I peered at the faces of the men carrying the god. They looked bored and sweaty! No joy or gladness, no thankfulness, no worship or hope, just sweat and strain. As they passed me, I didn't call out, for none of them looked like they'd want to stop and answer any questions.

Then I knew. The hope I had this morning died. The gods could not help me with Pater.

Crossing the Forum I headed back home. I glanced over toward the house of the Vestal Virgins. *It's because of the gods that Octavia is so unhappy! Draco told me she can't marry until she is forty years old. Nobody will want to marry her then.* I felt sadder for Octavia than ever. Then I began to feel sad for all of Rome. That's when I decided it's all right to laugh at the gods and sometimes even to hate them. *After all, they aren't real.*

Feeling low, I watched my feet carry me steadily out of the fancy marble area of Rome to our dilapidated insula.

Is there a real God? If there is a real God, just what is He like?

Then I remembered Rabbi Saul. He worshiped an invisible God. I wondered if his invisible God wore no clothes and sat around in an empty temple waiting for someone to bring him presents. I turned toward the rabbi's store hoping he wasn't too busy to talk.

But I saw the store was bustling with business when I got there.

"Why, Chezek, good morning! You're out early. Sit down and have a pickled egg!" Rabbi called out from the counter as he waited on a large woman.

She had her four children all lined up with their arms

full of groceries. "Rufus, don't drop those eggs. Come on, children; put it all up here so Saul can tell us how much we owe."

Rufus was my age, and sometimes we played together in the courtyard of his insula. He had a great ball-throwing arm. After he unloaded, he came over where I sat, and I offered him half of my egg.

He took it and said as he munched, "You friends with Saul? Why did he call you that funny name?

"We've lived here all my life, Ruf. He likes me so he gave me that name. It's Chezek. It has a secret meaning."

"My mater said they're Jews and have funny beliefs—they only believe in one God."

"How many does your mater and pater believe in?"

"We have to worship as many as we can, so Pater will be able to support our family. The gods are very jealous if we don't. If they get angry, we might starve. Mater says, unless we sacrifice to them, all of Rome could starve."

"Do you believe in them, Ruf?"

"I'm afraid to say."

"Why?"

"You know, Willem."

"Yes."

"Do you believe in them, Willem?"

"No."

"Why are you not afraid to say?"

"They're not real or alive. And my mater does not care."

"Oh. Will you tell me, Willem, if you ever find a good reason to believe in them?"

"Yes. But, I don't think there is one."

Just then Rufus' mater called him to help carry the groceries home. With his arms full, he stepped over to me and said, "Thanks for the egg, Willem."

Rabbi Saul was in between customers when they left. He walked over to where I sat.

"So, Willem, to what do I owe this morning visit? Do you need some more financial advice?" He wiped his old hands on his clean apron. His wrinkled face was one big smile. The grey beard that flowed over onto his apron bib was clean and curly.

I stood up and then felt shy. "I…uh…want to talk about… uh…your God," I said in a near whisper.

Rabbi's eyebrows shot up with surprise. He studied my face almost long enough to count my freckles. Then Rabbi Saul's eyes unexpectedly filled with tears, and he tenderly said, "What did you say, Chezek?"

Louder, I said, "Will you tell me about your God, Rabbi?"

"Oh, son, you don't mean that, do you?"

"Yes, sir. I have visited the temples of our gods this morning and found that they are not real. I remembered that your God is invisible. I would like to know about Him, if you could tell me. Is it a secret? Can you tell me, please?"

"What do you want to know, Willem?" Rabbi's face was very solemn.

"Does He wear clothes?"

Suddenly Rabbi burst out laughing. And I let go and laughed too—until my sides hurt!

When we both were able to quit, he said, "Chezek, come back this afternoon when business dies down. I want to show you something."

How curious I was as I went back to the cheese shop. Mater didn't need me, so I went over to Senny's. He was helping his mater clean their apartment.

She had a few words for me. "There you are, Willem, always getting my boy into some kind of trouble! He can't help but follow you around. I never know where you might go next!"

"Did you like your pretty shells, Mater Sophia?"

"Don't try it, Willem! Next time you have a scheme, please come and tell me about it first. I will at least know where my boy has gone for the day!"

"Yes, Mater. I will try."

I helped Senny carry out the rugs and we got busy beating the dust out of them.

"Mater did like the shells I gave her, Willem. She also knows about our plans for the money, and is interested in your plan."

"Senny, my mater told me I have a pater. I learned from Elise that he is coming back soon to Rome from Gaul. I hope he will also be interested in our plan."

"My pater is a soldier, too. I've never mentioned him before. I was afraid you wouldn't be happy that I had one and you didn't. My pater is stationed in Palestine. He writes to mater and sends her money. He used to live here in Rome."

"How did it work when he lived here?"

"All the time he had off from the army he came and spent with us. Though soldiers can't marry, they can visit anyone they please, just as long as they're loyal to the emperor."

"Do they get into trouble for having children?"

"I don't know. My pater was very careful. I never

approached him if I saw him away from our apartment."

We finished up the rugs and Senny's mater handed us some bread and olives. We were sitting on the steps enjoying them when Turk and Blue showed up.

"Too late to work, too late to eat," Senny commented.

Turk sat down and said, "I'm ready for another trip to the sea, are you two?"

"We'll go soon. Mater is coming this time. Your maters will be glad, especially yours, Senny."

Leo ran up and joined us. "I'm ready if you're talking about visiting the Great Sea again."

Blue, leaning on the rail, informed him, "Willem's mater is coming with us. Let your mater know. Then she won't worry."

"My mater doesn't ever worry about me. She's too busy with all the other children. I go where I want, when I want!" Leo bragged.

I said, "This time tell her, Leo. She might like it." Then I brushed the crumbs off my hands and tunic, and said, "Thanks for the food, Senny, and thank your mater for me. Right now I need to go see Rabbi Saul."

I took my time going to the store, looking into the faces of the people I passed on the street. Did the old woman with the curly grey hair and wrinkled face believe in the gods? A young slave hurrying somewhere glanced at me, and I thought about what kind of god he worshiped. I passed a shop selling household gods, the lars and penates that Turk and Blue's family worshiped. *Strange to worship something you bought.*

When I made it to the store, I could see business had slowed. Rabbi Saul saw me and motioned me to the back of the store. We went through a thick curtain to their family's storage and break room. I'd never been behind the curtain before.

We turned up some dark stairs and Rabbi Saul opened a door at the top. Sunlight streamed through a high window. The small room's floor was covered with a thick red carpet, and the walls were of some light and pretty wood. At the other end of the room was a cabinet built out of the same light wood sitting on a darker wooden table.

Rabbi motioned for me to come on in. "You asked me about my God. Willem, I will show you something that is the essence of my God. It is the Torah. It is the very words of God!" He used the word "Elohim" for God.

He went to the cabinet and opened it. Inside the handles of a large scroll stuck out from its shiny cloth wrapper. I looked at the scroll for a few moments then Rabbi Saul closed the cabinet door. He led me back out of the room and down the stairs. He sat down and motioned to the other chair. "Sit, Chezek."

I sat down and looked into his serious face.

He said, "My God is invisible. And He is holy. Do you know what that means, son? It means He does cover His nakedness, and He is always good and wise. And He is always present. When He sent our forefathers word that He was going to help us when we were slaves in Egypt, He called Himself, 'I AM THAT I AM.'"

"Is that what the scroll says?"

"Yes. It says long before that time He created all that is in this world, including all of us humans. It tells us that He has chosen a people to love and to be His peculiar treasure, and that is us Jews. It tells how He chose a Jew named Moses to give us His laws. And it informs us of His laws He expects us to keep."

"Does it tell you what He thinks about us Romans?"

"No, except it does speak of those who worship idols. He forbids that."

I sat there soaking up this idea of a God who speaks. It was what I was looking for today. Yet, the scroll was in the cabinet. Rabbi Saul had not offered to let me try to read it.

"Rabbi Saul, who else can read the scroll?"

"It is holy. It was given to us Jews. I may not offer it to you, but I will answer any question you would like to ask me."

I told the rabbi about my pater coming to Rome. I told him I wanted my pater to come live with me and love me. I asked him, "Does your God have any help for me about my pater?"

Rabbi Saul stroked his curly beard and looked at me. Then he said, "The Romans are now our masters. The scroll says that our God will send us another prophet like unto Moses, who will free us from such masters. Until He comes, we must obey the Romans."

"When He comes, will He help me?"

"He will help us Jews."

"So He wouldn't help me?"

"I-I don't know, Willem." Rabbi Saul let his eyes fall from mine then. He looked up at the rough ceiling of the storage room for a moment. When he looked back into my eyes, he said, "I will ask Him."

"How, Rabbi?"

"I pray to Him. I ask Him to help me and prosper my business. I ask Him to keep Simeon safe when he travels

the sea. I ask Him to keep us in favor with the Romans."
He lifted his eyes to the ceiling again. "I will ask Him about
your need, Willem."

"May *I* ask Him myself?"

"You could, but I don't know if He will hear or answer you."

"Then Rabbi Saul, will you ask Him for me, and will you
ask Him right now?"

"Why, Chezek? Do you believe in Him?"

"I don't know. But, I don't have a God. And I need one."

Instantly Rabbi Saul's eyes filled with tears. He came
over to me and hugged my shoulders to his white aproned
belly. "We will see, son, we will see."

I left feeling like I'd been to another world. How alone I was
outside of it now. *I wish I were your son or grandson, Rabbi.
For then your invisible God would help me.*

CHAPTER FIVE

LANEE'S WEDDING

L ANEE, radiant and waiting, was quietly perched on the stool by the door. She felt Deborah's hands gently rearranging one of her curls. It caused her to turn and smile at her friend, so elegant in her pink silk gown. More friends, Sarah, Elisabeth, and Misha, chattered nearby. Lanee looked around to make sure her eema and abba were there. She saw them on the bench holding hands with their heads together. They also were dressed in new linen finery.

The young bride smoothed the shiny silk skirt of her white wedding dress, thinking of last night. She and Eema had walked to the lake for the traditional bath before the wedding day. Like her dress, the Sea of Galilee shined in the light of the moon; and the water slid over her smooth and cool.

Soon Ben is coming for me! She couldn't help remembering her first sight of him walking by the well. *Ben! He brushed his hair away from his eyes and stared into mine. I was only twelve, but I knew I loved him. A year ago he asked me to be his wife. And tonight it's happening! Oh, Jesus, it's really happening. Thank you, thank you!*

She bowed her head over the beautiful silk veil in her hand. *And oh, help me, help me! I'm not even seventeen yet...I...I don't know how to be a wife, Lord.* She turned her head to look into Deborah's calm eyes. *My friend told me not to be afraid. Married to David only last month, and she is happier than I have ever seen her.*

Suddenly she heard a sound—happy voices heading her way. Laughter rang out again and again the closer they got. She listened as the pushing and shoving sounds grew louder. She recognized his voice. "Let go, my friends! I'm already late. Lanee's waiting for me!"

Footsteps shuffled up under the sycamore tree, followed by a light knock at the door.

She swallowed the lump in her throat. It had been a week since she'd seen him. She watched Abba walk to the door. Rising from the stool, she smoothed her skirt as the oaken door swung wide open.

Ben stepped in before her, tall and brown from the sun, clothed in a wedding garment of the finest black linen. His dark bushy hair lay tamed under a small cap over his crown. When she raised her eyes to his, a sweet smile curved his lips and lit up his face. "I…You're…lovely," he said.

"You…you are too, Ben."

Then everyone began talking at once.

"We must hurry," David urged, grinning happily at his friends.

Abba, looking a little teary, said, "Lead on, Ben, we're right behind you." He took Eema's arm and gently smiled down at her. Eema's tears fell quietly. She tried to smile back at him.

Ben led them over the dirt road to their new house on his abba's farm. Lanee walked beside him thinking of the many hours they'd spent together building their house. It was a two story stone house and had a courtyard out back just like Lanee's old home. She had helped Ben finish the oven out there the last time she'd seen him.

The courtyard now held something she'd not seen yet— it was their own *chuppah!* Their mothers had spent many hours joyfully decorating the special wedding tent. Lanee knew Brother Thaddaeus was near the chuppah waiting for them. *And the whole congregation will be out there watching for Ben and me.*

"Here they come!"

Lanee felt so shy she ducked her head. Then turning her head she peeked over at Ben, wondering how he was taking such attention. His dark eyes danced with joy. They caught hers and held them.

Oh, my! I feel as excited about him as I did back then by the well, and we didn't even know each other! Oh, Ben, today is our wedding day!

He squeezed her hand, and said out loud as if he'd heard her, "Let's enjoy it, Lanee!"

She was beginning to do just that.

The newlyweds David and Deborah each grabbed their hands and drew them toward the chuppah.

Before they entered the wedding tent, Ben stopped and took the veil from Lanee's hand. He did his best to fit it over her head and get it straight, sometimes allowing his eyes to meet with hers. Satisfied, he gently arranged the transparent silk over her face and shoulders. He stood before Lanee with his hands open, beholding her.

Everyone cheered. Under the veil, Lanee blushed.

Together they stepped into the tent. David and Deborah took hold of the tent poles beside them, and Yosef and Savta held the other two beside Brother Thaddaeus. Their parents stood outside the tent at their sides.

The service began. Brother Thaddaeus ben Tzadik, regal behind his curly red beard, spoke with solemn joy, "As Abraham and Sarah were joined as husband and wife in their tent, so Benjamin and Lanee are being joined today." He smiled at them through the tears that had suddenly sprung up into his green eyes. Lanee remembered his flowing tears when he'd repented and found Jesus. Ever since then she'd seen his tears often, for now his heart was so tender.

Brother Thaddaeus looked at Lanee and stepped back. She knew it was time to circle Ben. She took a turn around him once and met his eyes. Again and again she went, counting seven times, shyly catching his eyes each time she passed in front of him. Then she stopped by his side.

Brother Thaddaeus said, "Yes, Lanee, it is even as the church lives and moves around our Master, the Lord Jesus Christ, so the bride encircles her bridegroom." He looked out to the congregation and said, "Now, Lanee and Benjamin will bring you the bread and juice to share the Lord's Supper together. "

When they'd served everyone, Lanee and Ben took their places, and this time her abba began to pray, "Lord Jesus, you died on the cross, so we could be saved. You arose from the grave, and now you're in heaven praying for us every day. Will you bless our church to always circle around you, and will you bless our remembrance of your sacrifice on the cross?"

He motioned to the church and they all ate the little fragments of unleavened bread and took a small sip from the juice cups being passed around. Then Abba turned his whole attention to his daughter, the bride, and her groom. He prayed with tears in his voice, "Thank you for giving Benjamin and Lanee to each other, Lord Jesus. Bless them to tell others of your great love and salvation. May their marriage be blessed by you, God, our Father, our Lord Jesus Christ, and Holy Ghost, our Comforter? Amen."

Lanee looked over at her abba. His prayer had touched her heart, and for a moment, drew her attention away from the wedding. She thought of the boy.

Saviour, may I find Willem soon? I don't know where he is. Guide me to him. Then she remembered from now on she would be with Ben. *I mean guide us to him, Lord. We'll help him—we'll tell him about you.*

She turned and saw David's eema come up beside him. Their voices filled the courtyard as they sang,

"I take thee as my blessing,
I hold thee as my friend.
I marry thee my beloved,
I am thine, Amen.

Oh, joy, my joy!
Oh, love, my love!
I marry thee my beloved
I am thine, Amen.

I will help thee, my husband,
I will hold thee, my wife,
Jesus gave us to each other,
Jesus, Saviour, our life!

Oh, joy, my joy!
Oh, love, my love!
Jesus gave us to each other,
Jesus, Saviour, our life!"

As the last notes drifted away, Lanee's heartbeat sped up. She looked shyly into Ben's earnest eyes. Brother Thaddaeus took their hands and blessed them as he placed her beloved's on top of hers. "I now pronounce that Benjamin ben Jacob and Shira, and Lanee bat Jonathan and Priscilla are husband and wife."

Ben lifted her veil and took her into his arms. He held her close and kissed her. In the middle of her husband's first kiss, Lanee felt the nervous fear depart. Pure quiet joy came stealing into her heart. *Today I am surely the happiest girl in Galilee, for now I am Benjamin ben Jacob's wife!*

CHAPTER SIX
BENJAMIN'S DOVE

L ANEE hadn't known a thing about seasickness. Now she did.

"Jesus, please help my sister," Deborah said as she gently patted her back. Neither she nor David or Ben had gotten sick. Lanee was glad they hadn't had to lean over the rail, time after time, day after day, as she had. It was miserable and embarrassing.

Ben had been so kind to her, only laughing a little after the worst days were past, when she had managed a weak chuckle. It had taken the first shine off their marriage trip. Then she learned that a person *could* get over the awful nausea even while the ship still rolled over the waves.

Oh, thank you, Jesus, I'm feeling better. Still weak, she reclined against the pillow on the deck bench.

I never would have dreamed that I'd be on this ship ten days after my wedding. It had to be Jesus' plan that He'd inspired Dod Ethan to carry out. Surely his fine sandals will sell well in Rome. The ship was loaded with over five hundred pairs.

Lanee remembered how it all came together. Ben's sabba stood up at the wedding and said, "When I last saw my grandson in Caesarea, he told me of a lovely dove he hoped to catch for his own here in Arbela."

Everyone laughed at that.

"After he came back home, I bought a new ship, and

decided to call her *Benjamin's Dove.* I knew he would catch her!"

When the laughter died down, he turned toward them and held up his glass of spiced pomegranate juice, "To Lanee and Benjamin, may you be blessed with many little pigeons and with many years to love each other!"

Dod Ethan, Deborah's abba, Ben's sabba, Yosef, and Lanee's abba got their heads together as the party went on. Dod Ethan rose up to announce a surprise for Ben and Lanee, *and* David and Deborah. They were sending the two couples on a wedding trip to Rome. Ben's uncle, Dod Tobias, was the captain of the new ship. It would carry, along with the newlyweds, many styles of sandals, crates of dried figs and raisins from the farms, and even some other passengers to make it a profitable trip.

And we're carrying the good news of our Lord to the great city of Rome, Lanee thought, excitedly. *Oh, Lord Jesus, will I soon meet Willem?*

After Lanee's seasickness completely left, she explored the ship with Deborah. The first person she met was Dod Tobias' Egyptian wife Nalia. She was the ship's cook. Lanee and Deborah learned how to manage some of their girl things on board with her kind help. They volunteered to help her with meals. A crew of eight men, and ten other passengers, along with the six of them, had to eat every day.

Lanee had helped serve the morning meal and was freshening up afterwards in the cabin. Ben stuck his head through the door, "Isha, come up to the bow with me—Dod is teaching me how to steer the ship!"

She smiled both at his calling her *wife,* and how excited

he looked. "I'll catch up with you!" When she made her way to the bow, she realized she had learned to walk with the rolling of the ship. Her eyes turned up to the billowing triangular sail, then toward the choppy sea. A huge grain ship sailed ahead of them. They had followed it all the way from Ceasarea.

A cold wind cut across her. *I'm glad I tied my hair down.* She was wearing the many-colored scarf her grandmother had given her just before she left Arbela. Savta had hugged her and whispered, "I believe you will help many to learn of our Saviour, Granddaughter. I will be praying for you." Lanee also knew the church back in their village was praying for all of them.

When she stepped into the wheelhouse, she saw burly Dod Tobias standing beside Ben. Her Benjamin was at the wheel guiding the ship!

"Well, hello, Lanee. I'm glad to see you got past the sickness."

"Thank you, Dod. I love the trip now. Is Doda Nalia back in the galley? She might want some help."

"No, no, I'm leaving Benjamin to steer for awhile, and I know you can make him good company. I'll be in my cabin. Come and get me if you need me." When he was gone, she stood quietly behind Ben watching his hands on the wheel. She saw a smile curving his lips when he looked to the side. *It feels so good to be here alone with him.* She took a step closer.

He said without turning around, "We're really married, and we're really together on this ship."

"You are happy, dearest?" she said.

He reached his arm around and gathered Lanee up into its warmth. "I am finding my life is much more than ever I hoped it to be."

Lanee snuggled closer to him then asked, "Will we like Rome, Ben? I've heard that it is big and wicked."

"We are going for Jesus; that I know. He will take care of us."

"I keep thinking Willem is there. He's so real to me, though I've only seen him that one time."

"What do you think Jesus wants you to do when you meet him in person?"

"I think we will all be friends. I think he will listen when I tell him about Jesus."

"I wonder why his face was sad when you saw him."

"I don't know. Maybe Rome is not a happy place."

"We will be there in another two weeks, if all goes well. Let's pray for Willem and for our mission to the people of Rome as we travel. I'll get with David, and you and Deborah pray together. Remember how God has moved in Arbela. Rome may be big and wicked, but our God is much bigger and His goodness can overcome any wickedness that comes against Him."

Lanee looked up into his tan face, and said, "They've probably not heard of Jesus. Should we preach on the streets, or maybe we should go to the Jews first? What do you think Jesus would do in Rome, Ben?"

"He would heal their sick. He would testify of His being sent from His Father! He would show them the scars in His hands and feet. He would *help* them believe in Him, Lanee, like He did me!"

"And me, too. I remember Him opening my heart to the touch of God. He would!"

"Pray, my dove, that we can be His power in Rome. Pray that the Romans can meet Jesus through us!"

"And, my Ben, pray that when I meet Willem, he'll be drawn to Jesus."

"I will. I can't help but wonder what kind of boy would cause Jesus to give you that vision?"

"A very unusual boy," Lanee said as she looked out toward the wild sea. "How will we find him in such a city? I don't think he is Jewish. But neither did he really look Roman. What if he isn't living in Rome?"

"I don't doubt he is there, Lanee," Ben said. "Jesus has led us too clearly toward Rome for me to doubt that."

She was glad to hear it. *How good it is to have such a friend to spend my life with.* She leaned closer against him and said, "I am excited to see the capital of the world, but I have heard the emperor is an unpredictable and perhaps unstable man. What do you think he might think of our preaching Jesus to the Romans?"

"I have also heard he doesn't live in Rome, but on the island of Capri, many miles from the city. Perhaps our month in Rome will not be of any concern to him."

"Oh, if he only wanted to know about Jesus, and could cause all of Rome to turn to Him!"

Ben seemed to study the rolling sea ahead before he answered her, "We can pray, Lanee! We can pray."

CHAPTER SEVEN
WILLEM MEETS LANEE

MATER and Julian liked each other immediately. She offered him three denarii to take all of us to Ostia, which really upped her in his estimation. We had gathered some large burlap bags, and ended up taking Elise along, after her mater begged mine to let her go. I still didn't want to take her, but I was out of the decision.

You should have seen Mater's face when we made the turn from Rome west toward the sea. The first whiff of fresh air caused her to pull the pins out of her hair, and let it fly behind her. I'd never known her to do such a thing. My four partners didn't know what to think about my mater joining us anyhow…it wasn't exactly *motherly*.

I saw Julian eyeing Mater. I guess he didn't get to see many mothers, since he spent most of his life on his boat.

Mater lived most of her life in the cheese shop. "Mater,

put your hat on." I said coming up beside her. I was glad she bought that straw hat from Rabbi Saul.

"I should have bought a hat for you, Willem."

"It's all right, I'm used to the sun. Did Elise bring one?"

"Yes, her mater sent a whole bag of clothes and things for her to change into if she gets wet."

"If? If? Mater, her mother sure doesn't know Elise very well."

When she heard her name, Elise came sauntering over the deck to us. She'd irritated me with that smug expression ever since Mater agreed to let her go.

I had to do something about that face. "Go dig your hat out of that clothes bag you brought and put it on!" I ordered.

After first narrowing her big brown eyes at me, she turned to do it.

"Willem, look, we must be nearing Ostia. There's a huge building up ahead," Mater pointed out.

"It's the grain warehouse." Then I clamped my mouth shut.

Mater turned and gazed into my eyes. "What else did you explore the last time you came, son?"

Just then Julian called out, "Look, up ahead!"

Slaves were hauling three impressive barges up the river toward us. The first barge bristled with the spears of many soldiers. We passed pretty close, so I tried to look at the men's faces. Was one of them my own pater? Mater had turned her back on them.

Julian suddenly cried, "Down on your knees—it's the emperor! It's Tiberius!" We all obeyed, bowing our heads too. As we passed, I caught a glimpse of an old man with a silver circlet around his balding head. He watched everything from his golden chair perched on the deck between two muscled soldiers.

Slowly up the river the old man went. He was followed by another barge of soldiers. I jumped up and scanned as many faces as I could. Mater stood up beside me. I turned to her and realized she wasn't looking their way. Her long dark hair was blowing behind her, and she had her eyes closed.

Why isn't Mater looking for Pater? She didn't say anything the day I told her he was coming back to Rome. She only cried with me. Why?

The barge slipped past us, and I was disappointed. Our two vessels moved farther apart. Suddenly one of the soldiers in the back of the barge whipped around to stare. He started to raise his spear to wave then pulled it back down in the middle of the gesture. The distance was too great...*was he beginning to wave at Mater and me? Was that Lucius Dio? Was that Pater?* I strained as hard as I could to see the tiny figure still staring back at us.

"M-Mater. I think it was Pater. I think he recognized you and me. M-Mater, did you see him?"

She shook her head. Then she stood up, balled up her hair under her hat, and without a backward glance toward the barge, said, "Look, I can see the Great Sea!"

She's not going to answer me. Does she not care if it was Pater?

"Mater, did you see him?" I asked again, louder this time.

"Don't, Willem!"

"Mater, It *was* Pater, wasn't it?"

"Stop it, Willem! You and I must make it on our own. Your pater will not want us to cause him trouble when he gets to Rome. He will work for the emperor, and we cannot be a hindrance to him."

I felt my face go red. "Me? ...a *hindrance*...to my father?"

"Oh, son, I'm sorry to put it so straight to you," Mater said, placing her arms around me, "but I need you to understand. Your pater cannot acknowledge us as his family. I will not be the cause of his losing his position in the army." She stared into my eyes with tears gathering in hers. Then she let go and dried her eyes on her sleeve. "Now, let us forget what you saw, and let's attend to those valuable shells."

I was still reeling from that word, *hindrance.* It was sticking in my heart like a sharp knife. I turned back toward the barge, now almost out of sight. Fighting back tears, I vowed, *Lucius Dio...I will meet you soon, and then I, your own son Willem, will not be a hindrance to you—I will help you, my pater!*

Julian let us out at the dock this time before the boat sailed out into the sea. Mater and Elise were chattering about the sea gulls and the waves crashing in. I didn't want to talk to anyone, but Blue walking beside me kept talking excitedly about the emperor's barge.

"Did you see all the flags and the beautiful serving girls lined up around the rail? Did you see the huge ring on his hand?"

Leo piped up, "He sure is old and ugly! I wouldn't want to be the emperor, if I had to look like him!"

Even I laughed at that.

We soon were crunching over the sand of the beach. With a loud "whoopee!" my fraters went running to the surf. Then I heard Elise's high-pitched cry, and was amazed to hear Mater's "Weeee!" as they ran toward the inviting waves holding hands.

They screamed and played, while I moved on down the beach looking most of all for the valuable abalone shells. Sure enough, as I walked farther and farther from the mouth of the river, the shells were abundant. By the time everyone else came dragging their sacks, I had found a dozen beautiful mother-of-pearl glazed abalone, and some other perfect shells that had sold well last time.

Mater exclaimed over every shell she found! She picked up some delicate brown shells that looked like fans, carefully piling them up on the beach. When her sack was almost full, she placed them on top of the sturdier ones. She loaded her stola with many miniature shells, crying out every time she found a new treasure. Even though my heart was sore, I enjoyed hearing her little cries of pleasure more than just about anything I'd ever listened to.

It didn't take a long time to fill up all our sacks.

"Mater, we can leave our sacks behind this palm tree, and go into town for some food. Maybe we'll see a boat heading to Rome after that."

She must have felt hungry too, for she quickly agreed. My friends were used to Mater being with us by then, and were enjoying her as much as Elise was. She paid for everything when we ordered our bean pastes and grape juice at the first shop we came to. We walked around Ostia letting our clothes dry on us.

Elise said, "When I get home, I'm going to tell all my friends that *I* saw the emperor's barge. It was only a few feet away from me. I could have almost touched His Highness!"

"Just don't give them any ideas of coming with us next time, Elise."

She frowned at me; then remembering something, she looked happy again. "I'll go with you to the Forum to sell my shells, and I'll be rich!"

I groaned. Elise was sure becoming a pest.

We strolled through the streets of Ostia. Mater was interested in the shops. "Oh, look! It's a cheese shop." We stayed outside as she went in to look around. She came out with a sample of goat cheese for us to try.

"I want to get some of this for my shop. The owner here said he gets it from Egypt, and I can buy some from him the next time I come."

Blue said, "Mater, will you come with us again next time? Our mater was not afraid for us to come when she heard you were coming too."

Turk chimed in, "You're our traveling Mater!"

Mater said, "Well, first we've got to find our way back to Rome today. What shall we do about that, Willem?"

"Last time Simeon came along and took us there." *I could only hope for him today!*

We went down to the docks where several ships were tied up. Some were loading, and others were unloading. I was amazed to see a familiar face.

"Hello, Cassius! Which ship are you working on?" He was a freedman I'd met at the Flavius villa when I'd delivered cheese there.

"Willem! You're in Ostia! Where will I see you next?" Cassius was a strong Italian, with dark curly hair falling over his brow. His tunic was sweat-stained and his beard had droplets of sweat dripping off of it. "I'm helping to unload this grain ship, the *Bountiful,* now, but this evening I will return to Rome on a small merchant ship, *Benjamin's Dove,* heading here from Palestine.

"How do you know this small ship will arrive then?"

"The master of the *Bountiful* hired me to guide the captain of the small ship into a safe place close to Rome. The people who are sailing the ship have never been to Rome before."

"We need a passage back to Rome tonight. Could we go with you? This is my mater and my friends. There will be seven of us."

Mater said, "If you could get permission from the captain, I would be glad to pay him for our passage. We will also be carrying some bags with us."

Cassius smiled at Mater then said "I will talk to the captain, dear lady. Will you be waiting somewhere I can find you?"

"Yes," I said, "we will be down on the beach near the mouth of the river."

Cassius said, "I will find you, either way."

We all went down to the beach. After making sure our bags were still behind the palm tree, we stretched out on the sand.

I curled up on my side and watched the waves come in, thinking. The word, *hindrance,* crossed my mind. I decided not to think about it and soon fell asleep.

I awoke at the sound of Cassius' stout sandals crunching over the sand toward us. The afternoon sun was about to sink into the water. I was lying up against Mater. When I rose up to see who was coming, I saw she had her arm protectively covering Elise.

"Ho! Willem!" He called out, waking everybody else up. "Captain Tobias said he'd carry you to the city. We need to get on back to the dock!"

Hurriedly brushing at the sand that covered our clothes, we grabbed our sacks and trudged after him. The afternoon breeze off the water felt good.

Mater came up beside me and said in a low voice, "Son, when we get there, let me talk to the Captain. He might not want to deal with an eleven-year-old boy."

"I know how to make friends, Mater."

"I understand. Yet we don't know whom we're dealing with."

"Cassius would have warned us off if he thought he was dishonest."

"Yes, I believe you're right. Still, let me do the talking."

I nodded.

Turk whistled as we neared the dock, "This ship's a beauty! Looks like a new one." Not like many of the old tubs we saw in Rome, this ship had new sails, new ropes, and even her crew looked neat and clean—they were all dressed up in matching tunics with handkerchiefs tied around their tanned foreheads.

Captain Tobias, wearing a wide leather girdle around his broad middle, called to us in Hebrew to come aboard. Smiling through his curly beard, he welcomed us in halting Greek. I asked Mater if I could speak with him in Hebrew. She cautioned me only to interpret for her and the captain.

"We are pleased to meet you, Captain." I said, bowing to him. "I know your language and will be glad to interpret for you."

His eyes measured me as he said, "Well, son, and how is

it that a fine Roman boy like you knows Hebrew?"

"I have Jewish friends who talk with me."

That's when Mater pulled my sleeve.

"This is my eema, who would like to speak with you through me."

After they agreed upon a price for our passage, Captain Tobias bid us to follow him to our seats for the journey upriver. He led us to a narrow bench near the middle of the ship.

"Will this suit your needs?"

"Yes, sir. Do you have any food we can purchase aboard? We haven't eaten since early today."

"Yes, I will send you some." Then he added kindly, "But it will be included in the price you paid."

I told the boys what he said and they all let out a cheer. Elise understood, for her mater was a Jew. I knew Mater understood a little Hebrew too, for she often shopped in Rabbi Saul's store. Language had never been a barrier for me; I picked it up just by listening to others talk. I was feeling very glad for that today.

Soon we saw a crew of men, naked to the waist, flinging ropes to the ship to pull it up the Tiber. I don't mind working when I have to, but I knew I wouldn't want to be one of those men. Their backs soon were glistening with sweat as they chanted and pulled in time. I was glad to be able to just sit and be pulled along.

We were standing by the rail watching everything when a teenage girl came toward us bringing a tray of food. She was pretty with long brown hair done up in a bright scarf. She handed me my cup of juice, so I turned to thank her. When her eyes met mine, she jumped with a start.

Not understanding, I just said thank you and gave her my best friendly smile.

She grinned back, still looking like I had somehow shocked her.

"I've heard that you speak my language," she said as she handed Mater her juice. "My name is Lanee. What's yours?"

"It's Willem."

Suddenly she gave out a little shout, kind of like, "Whee!" She lifted both hands and cried into the sky, "Oh, thank you, Jesus! Thank you, Father! Oh, thank you, Holy Ghost!" Then she danced—that's all I could call it—she danced all around us and clapped her hands!

Shocked, I whispered to Mater. "What kind of people are *these* Jews? Rabbi Saul never acted like this."

Then the girl ran away. We sat down to eat, wondering.

Soon she came back. A young man was with her, who stared at me as he approached.

"This is my husband, Ben," she said when they reached us. "Will you tell *him* your name?"

"W...well, yes. It's Willem."

Then they both lost all sense. He danced and clapped, yelling thanks to someone he called Jesus, as Lanee raised her hands and cried out the same words she'd been yelling before. Then they both ran off.

Mater said around the bread she was chewing, "Some really strange people. Why are they so glad to know your name, son?"

I shook my head and said, "Maybe they like that name."

I ate a sweet fig, thinking, *What will happen next?*

I didn't have long to wait, for Lanee and Ben returned

bringing another couple. These two could have been models for the marble gods in Rome. He had curly black hair, and she was the most beautiful girl I'd ever seen.

Lanee said, "These are my friends, David and Deborah. Will you please tell them your name?"

I laughed, and said really loud, as if they'd been hard of hearing, "It's Willem, I tell you!"

Well, that was the worst thing I could have done, for all four of them started dancing and shouting, and even talking in a language I didn't understand! (What new language was that?)

By that time Mater's eyes were like saucers, and all the boys and Elise were ready to run away. I motioned them to stay really still. Maybe the fit they were having would die down if we didn't move or say anything else.

Sure enough in a few moments they all quieted down and came back to stare at me.

"Why are you staring at me?" I asked.

Lanee said, "I've seen you before."

"Have you been to Rome before now?"

She looked very pleased when she said, "No."

"Then, where did you see me? I've lived in Rome all my life."

"I saw you in my mind," she said, again smiling as if she knew a sweet secret that I didn't know.

"Oh," I said, like I knew just what she meant.

"Jesus showed you to me."

"Oh." *Who is this Jesus?*

They just stood there staring at me. I wanted to say something back to them, but I couldn't think of just what.

Finally Lanee's husband said, "Now we will leave you to

eat your meal in peace. But, may we come back later and talk to you again?"

I remembered how Rabbi Saul spoke of His invisible God. They were Jews too. Perhaps this Jesus had something to do with their invisible God. I really *did* want to ask them about that, so I answered, "Yes, do."

Chapter Eight

Do You Know Jesus?

WE were glad to see the ship land at the same dock Julian used. Cassius helped us off, saying, "Captain Tobias was happy to have seen you safely back to Rome. He wanted me to tell you he hopes to see you again before the ship sails back to Palestine."

"When will that be, Cassius?"

"I'm not sure. If I find out, I'll come by the cheese shop."

Mater said, "We thank you for your help. When you come by, I'll reward you with some of my best cheese."

Cassius' mouth twisted up into the nicest smile I'd ever seen him give. His rough face shone down on Mater and she gave him her sweet smile back. Mater was doing very well outside of the cheese shop. I was really proud of her.

Then he left us on the dock to go back to work. The sun was almost down when we picked up our bags and headed into town.

"What a haul of shells, Willem!" Leo exclaimed as we lugged them home. "Let's go to the market tomorrow and sell them!"

At first I didn't answer him. My mind was on the encounter on the deck of Benjamin's Dove. *The girl Lanee and the other three didn't come back to talk to me. I wonder if I'll ever see them again. How glad they were to see me!*

"What do you say, Willem?" Turk said. "Want to see how many denarii we can collect tomorrow?"

I shook the memory of that pretty girl dancing all around me out of my head and answered, "Yes, we'll go in the morning. Mater, may we take yours and sell them at the same time?"

"Yes. But, son, what about the abalone shells the man from the Praetorian camp wanted?"

"I'll take them in a sack. Maybe he'll show up tomorrow, and if he doesn't I'll take them to the camp later." I knew we had a good number of them. At ten denarii apiece, we'd need a bigger pouch to hold our money. I was hoping if I went to the camp I might see Pater, though I didn't know how I would recognize him.

Wearily we finally turned down our overcrowded street. Mater took Elise to her door, while I carried both our sacks to ours. The others waved as they dropped off at their apartments. I waved back absent-mindedly.

Lanee, Ben, David, Deborah—all Jews who know the invisible God! I do want to see them again. I've never met anyone like them…I've never seen such happy eyes in anyone's face. And who is Jesus?

~~~

"Willem, Willem! Get up and come help me!" Mater called up to me the next morning.

I got dressed and ran down the stairs. I was surprised at the early morning customers she had. Mater gave me a knife and pointed to an old man who was sniffing around near the goat cheese.

"Good morning, sir. Would you like to have a taste?"

He picked up a round cheese and handed it to me. "I'm looking for the sweet and salty cheese like I used to make in Greece. If that's it, I'll buy that one and two more!"

"We get many of our cheeses from Athens, sir." I handed him a white sliver, and he took a bite.

I turned to cut a slice for another customer then came back to him.

"No... no, that's not it," he said, continuing to chew. "I was hoping."

"How about this yellow one? I have a Greek friend who buys this one regularly. He says it reminds him of home."

The old man waited for me to slice off some, then tasted it. "It's not like what I made, but it does taste good. I'll take it."

While I rewrapped the cheese the old man watched me. "Say, young man, do you know anyone by the name of Jesus?"

My head snapped up and I looked into his watery eyes. *That's the name Lanee was shouting out yesterday!*

"I...I've heard the name. In fact I heard of that name just yesterday. But I don't know who He is. Do you know Him?"

"I've seen Him." He handed me a coin, and I gave Him change from the till. He thanked me then said, "I saw the man before I came to Rome. It was in Jerusalem where I was peddling some silk tunics in the market. That's my profession. I was standing in the market when this Jesus came walking through with a whole crowd following Him. He seemed to be close to thirty or so. A Jew He was. Since I had already sold my merchandise, I decided to follow the crowd and see what the man was doing."

"Sir, I really want to hear this. Can you hold on just a moment while I wait on another customer?"

"Sure, son."

I hurried and sold the woman her cheese, put the money in the till, and came back to him. "Then what happened?"

"As I was saying, I started following the young man. He left the market with the whole crowd behind Him. I hurried around on another street to get ahead of them, so I could really see Him. When I got there, he had stopped right in front of one of the beggars leaning against the wall. I thought he was going to give him some money. But He reached down and picked the man up. The man's eyes were all white—for he was blind. I saw Jesus bend down, pick up some dirt, and spit on it. He mixed it up then began to coat the blind man's eyelids.

"'Go wash in the pool of Siloam,' He said.

"I decided to follow the blind man to see what would happen. He must have known the way, for he hardly stumbled at all. When he knelt down and splashed water on his face, I watched.

"The white was gone from his eyes! I'm telling you the truth, son. His eyes looked as clear as your young green ones. He whooped out, 'I can see!' and then started back to where he'd seen Jesus.

"I followed him back, but Jesus was gone."

"Did you see any more of Jesus?"

"No. And I had to get aboard my ship, so I left for Caesarea. But I've been asking everyone I see if they know Him. Maybe I'll get to hear some more about this person who has such power. When I go back, I'm going to try to find Him."

"Will you wait just a moment until I can tend to this customer? I'll be right back. I think I may be able to help you."

I sliced a nice piece of soft goat cheese for the customer, and while she was trying it, I came back to the man.

"Sir, yesterday a girl I met from Palestine mentioned His name to me. If I see her again, I'll tell her you're interested in talking to her. May I ask your name and where she can find you?"

The old man's eyebrows lifted and his eyes glistened. "I'm Philip of Macedonia. I will come back each day while I'm in Rome. Maybe I can talk to the girl."

"Uh...Philip, sir...how do you think the man Jesus made the blind man's eyes to see?"

The old man picked up his cheese and packed it under his arm. As he turned toward the street, he said, "He must be a god!"

CHAPTER NINE

ROME!

OD Tobias and Doda Nalia escorted the two couples to the *Lex Roma,* an elegant inn adjacent to the Forum Romanum. They were being treated to luxurious rooms by both sides of the family and Yosef. The plan was to get them settled in their suites, and then allow them a whole month to explore Rome. During that month Dod Tobias would take *Benjamin's Dove* to Greece and pick up a load of olive oil to sell before heading home.

When Lanee entered the room, all she could do was exclaim, "Oh, my, I love it!" The pale blue curtains airily brushed the tile floor across from a large bed with a coverlet designed from the same shimmering blue fabric. A tray of sweets and a dark blue jar of drink awaited them on the low table between the windows.

She shrugged off her light woolen cloak onto the bed and examined the walls adorned with scenes from a garden, complete with deer, sheep, and even fish in the pond. Her simple room in Arbela seemed so far away.

No, it was hers *and* Ben's room before they had left for Rome. The last few days after the ceremony her parents had welcomed Ben into their home as their son. It was wonderful how right it felt for him to be there with them!

"Benjamin, would you prepare the message for our service next week?" Abba had asked one night after supper. "Brother

Thaddeaus and I believe it would bless the young people to hear it."

Ben looked startled. Then he said, "Yes, Abba, the Lord has already given me a topic. Did you know Jesus has shown me that I am to preach His Word?"

Abba proudly declared, "Yes, son. He wants you to begin here, and I'm sure he'll use you in Rome. And I don't know where else you may be called to carry the gospel."

Ben had reached over for Lanee's hand. She looked at him with joy shining in her eyes.

"I will pray for you, son," Eema said. "I know Jesus will always show you what to say."

Just thinking of her father and mother way back across the sea made Lanee's heart suddenly ache with homesickness. *Abba and Eema are probably thinking of me just now, too. Jesus, please let them know I'm all right, and that they also are in my thoughts.*

Ben came in loaded down with the rest of their bags. He dropped them on the floor with a relieved sigh then looked toward her. Seeing the sad look on her face, he moved to her and without a word took her in his arms.

Lanee gazed up into his dark eyes and felt her heart relaxing from the tightening grip of loneliness. *It's our wedding trip! We'll not be gone long. It will be the adventure we'll tell our children about.*

Again she felt the shiver of excitement about their trip. "What shall we do first, Ben?"

"I've been praying about that, Lanee. If we ask the Holy Ghost to guide our steps, I know He'll show us." He loosened his hug, and let his hands rest on her arms. "I've been thinking about the Lord opening the door for us to come to the capital of the world on our wedding trip; also about how He's led us to Willem on the *Dove*. Surely His hand *is* with us."

Walking over to the window he gazed down on the crowds strolling around the Forum just beneath their room. "We may be the first people here that know anything about Jesus. We may be here to tell the Romans for the first time that God sent His Son to save them."

Lanee walked over and snuggled under his arm. She turned her eyes up to his and asked, "Should we seek out the Jews, Ben? Though Jesus preached to the Jews, He said to go into all the world and preach the gospel to every creature. Remember when He saved Brother Zibeon?"

"Yes, you're right, Yona. Let's put our things away, then let's find David and Deborah's room and ask them to pray with us for God's direction."

Lanee heard Ben use Abba's name for her, though Ben had changed Abba's Yonina, *(little dove)* to Yona *(dove)*. It was his sweet name for her ever since they'd left home. *Benjamin ben Jacob, you always do such lovely things to please me—surely that's why Jesus gave you to me!*

They hurried to put the room in order then set out hand in hand to find David and Deborah. They didn't have far to go, for when they passed the next door they heard David's happy laugh. Ben rapped on the door, and David opened it sweeping his arm out for them to enter. "Welcome to our palace, friends."

Deborah grabbed Lanee's hand and whispered, "Lanee, we're really in *Rome!* Did you ever think that you and I would

85

be in this great city, in this elegant inn, with our own wonderful husbands?"

Lanee could only smile and nod. Deborah had been such a different person since Jesus had saved her and David had fallen in love with her. *Oh, thank you, Lord Jesus, for my friend Deborah.*

David said, "Let's go see the sights! We can find something to eat while we're looking around."

"Wait, wait! David, let me tell you what Lanee and I have been discussing." Ben placed his hand on David's shoulder and looked at him soberly. "Haven't you seen that God's hand is with us, especially when He sent Willem to us? I think if we ask His direction in everything we do, He'll guide us. Do you agree?"

David ran his fingers through his curly dark hair and said, "I guess I let the excitement of actually being here overwhelm me. I'm sorry, everyone. Let's do slow down and pray."

He took hold of Deborah's hand. "Oh, Jesus, forgive me for caring for anything more than I do you! You've been so great a Saviour to me!" Then with tears in his eyes, he said to Ben, "Dear brother, thank you for your good counsel."

A thoughtful look crossed Ben's tanned face. "I think we're all going to be overwhelmed here at times. We must guard each other. Next time, David, it might be me that needs you to remind me of the Lord in the midst of this strange land. Lanee, will you and Deborah watch with us, too?"

Deborah holding tightly to David's hand with both of hers, nodded. Tears glistened in her eyes, for she had also felt the allure of Rome.

Lanee spoke up beside Ben, "David, let's ask the Lord

to order our steps and give us joy."

David remembered how Lanee had shared the day of Pentecost with him in Jerusalem, after they'd journeyed there together. How he'd met Deborah after moving to Arbela to be near Lanee and her family. What a special friend she'd been to him. He smiled at her and answered, "That's just what we need!"

It probably was the first time this luxurious room was used for such an event. Perhaps for the first time under the expansive tile roof of the *Lex Roma,* and most likely for the first time ever on any of the seven hills of the great crowded city of Rome, the capital of the world, four young believers in Christ fell to their knees and prayed for His help.

And soon their prayer would be answered!

CHAPTER TEN

THE VOICE IN THE FORUM

W E were all set up, and it was still early. Mater even let us bring some cheeses to sell. *After today I should be able to add a nice sum to our money sack.*

"Willem, Leo and I are going to chalk up some business." Senny held up the soft hunk of limestone then turned toward the entrance ways of the Forum. Instead of "Titius was here" or "Demetrius is a black dog!" Senny's idea was to draw an arrow to our booth proclaiming, "Shells from the Great Sea for sale!"

The Forum streets began to fill up with shoppers. I was busy helping a little girl spend her few sesterces on something pretty, when I saw Nicholas slowly making his way through the crowd to us. He seemed not as distressed as he was the last time.

The girl took her handful of butterfly shells and skipped back to her mater as Nicholas approached me.

"Well, Willem, I see you've been back to the sea. Did you find any abalone this time?"

I smiled into his sharp eyes, and said, "Yes sir, I did. Would you like to see them?"

His cough started. When it stopped, he nodded.

I grabbed the sack from behind our display and held it open for him to examine. His eyes narrowed as he saw the number and beauty of the shells we had gathered. "How many do you have?"

"I believe there are twenty, sir."

When he looked up into my eyes, I could see he was pleased. He put his hand on my arm and said, "Son, will you bring these to the camp tomorrow? If you will, I will give you the money then. Don't show them to anyone else, for I will buy them all. Is that understood, Willem?"

"Yes, sir."

Then he left.

Two hundred denarii! Two hundred denarii! We will need a larger bag to hold our money! I couldn't wait to tell Mater. I did wait to tell the other boys. We had a lot more selling to do today.

Turk and Blue were helping me, but when it seemed that all the wives in Rome wanted to see our shells, Senny and Leo stepped up and gave us a hand. We had sold all our cheese, and were down to the last few butterfly shells and sea fans, when we heard a voice raised over the crowd.

It took me a moment to realize the words being spoken were not in Latin, nor even in Greek, but the speaker was calling out three sentences in the Hebrew language.

"I am here to tell you some good news! The Saviour has come. His name is Jesus Christ!"

The voice was a young man's. I sought to see where it was coming from. Everyone else was searching for him too. Finally I saw a bushy-haired young man standing on the top step of Julius Caesar's temple. He opened his mouth and out came the same Hebrew words. He must have known all of us were listening then, for the Forum had grown quiet.

Then another young man appeared beside him. He began to sing a beautiful song in Hebrew. It said, "The Lord is my Shepherd, I shall not want..."

We all listened. I knew the people did not understand the words, but they listened to the beautiful voice as one. When the song ended, the first young man called out again, "We are here to tell you some good news! The Saviour has come. His name is Jesus Christ!"

The two young men then ran down the steps and immediately became part of the swarming crowd.

I knew them. It was Lanee's husband and his friend.

The Forum grew noisy again. We sold everything, and began gathering up our bags and blankets. I picked up the bag of money and smiled at the others, "We'll soon be able to buy our way out of Rome, brothers!"

Leo said, "We can have a horse to ride and a cow to milk!"

Turk joined in, "And a boat to catch fish from our own lake."

"And we'll smell clean air, and hear the hoot-owl every night," I added.

We had turned toward our poor streets after leaving the Forum. We always passed the temple of the Vestal Virgins. I remembered how I wanted to take the Virgin Octavia with us when we found our new home. Maybe the next time I brought cheese to Draco, I'd have a chance to speak to her. Would she want to go?

The streets were not quite as crowded as we left the temples and Forum behind. I couldn't help thinking about the message that Ben had called out in the Forum. "His name is Jesus Christ!" he'd said. Where were they now? I needed to find them. I left my friends at our insula and headed toward

Rabbi's store to give him the moneybag.

When I stepped into the door, there was Lanee, standing by the pomegranates, smiling at me as if she knew I were coming.

"It's you, Willem!"

Just as pretty as I remembered her on the ship, she walked up to me in Rabbi Saul's store. Her colorful scarf framed her excited face. Again it seemed I was some valuable treasure she'd happened upon. It made me feel shy.

"Hello, Lanee."

"We have met Rabbi Saul, and he says you are a friend of his. How Jesus is working!"

Just then Ben and their friends walked up from the back of the store.

"Do you remember my husband, Ben, and our friends, David and Deborah?"

"I saw and heard Ben and David today at the Forum."

"You did? Were you there shopping?"

"No, I was there selling. We sold our shells we brought from the sea."

"There were so many people there. We hoped that someone in the crowd would understand our language."

"I did."

"What did you think?"

"David can really sing. Ben's voice carries far."

"What did you think about what I said?" Ben asked.

"I was surprised. But I have heard the name of Jesus from someone else besides you. Yesterday a salesman visiting Rome came in my eemas' cheese shop and spoke of Him to me."

Lanee's face lit up. "Was he from Palestine and had he

met Jesus?"

"His name was Phillip of Macedonia. He wants to meet you. I'll let him explain to you why. He promised to come back each day to the shop in case I find you."

"Where is your eema's shop?" David asked, "We will come there to meet him."

Just then Rabbi Saul joined us. He said, "So, Chezek, you have met our friends from my homeland. They are from the hometown of my dear friend Yosef, whose abba was eminently learned in the scriptures. They will be in Rome for a month. We are going to worship our God this evening after the store closes. Would you and your eema like to come?"

"Yes, I would. Right now, Rabbi Saul, I want to show them where Eema's shop is."

"Certainly. All of you go ahead. I will prepare a meal for you young people so you may eat when you return. Chezek, I will see you later this evening. Be sure to give your eema my invitation."

"Rabbi Saul, may I speak to you alone for a moment?"

We stepped to the back of the store, where I gave him the moneybag for safekeeping.

He asked, "Do you know how much you have now?"

I shook my head and said, "Tomorrow after I sell the rest of our shells, could we count it up and see?"

"Yes, that will be a good time to do it."

We all walked down the street together to my insula. The streets, as usual, were crowded. When they could, Ben and Lanee walked on either side of me, with David and Deborah following.

Ben asked as he came up beside me again, "Willem, do

you work in your eema's shop when you're not selling your shells at the Forum?"

"Yes, but only when she needs me."

"Would you like to work for us when you're not busy?"

"What would I be doing for you?"

Just then a crowd of people met us going the other way, and we had to walk in single file.

When they passed, he and Lanee caught up, and he said, "Would you be willing to interpret what we say in Hebrew into Latin or Greek, whichever would fit the situation?"

I saw a sparkle in Ben's dark eyes when he asked me this. I turned to Lanee, and there it was again—that feeling of being special to her.

"Will you be speaking at the Forum as you did today?" Just the thought of raising my voice to all those grown-ups scared me! "I'm only eleven. Maybe they won't listen to me."

"Maybe they'll listen *because* you are only eleven." Deborah suggested from behind. Everyone laughed. She said, "Willem, my abba knew we would need an interpreter when we came here, and he sent enough money with me to pay you ten denarii for each time you help us. Do you think you can do it for that?"

I remembered the sound of Ben's voice in the Forum then imagined my voice interpreting his words. It was scary to think of. As we kept moving through the crowded street, a sweet thought of having my own land somewhere *outside* of Rome—maybe much sooner than I ever expected—came to me.

"I'll do it," I said, just before I felt the fear creeping back over me.

~~~

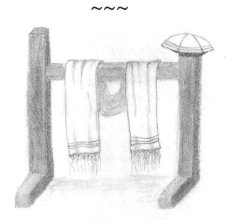

Rabbi Saul looked different wearing his prayer shawl and skullcap. It was the first time I'd seen him like this, for I'd never been invited before. Jews from all over Rome had gathered in Rabbi Saul's insula. I never knew the apartments of most of the second floor were gutted to produce a large meeting room. Almost every seat was taken when we arrived.

I was glad Mater came with me. She'd enjoyed seeing Lanee and the others again at the shop. When they relayed Rabbi Saul's invitation, she was both surprised and pleased. And guess who else was there?—bratty Elise! She saw me come through the door and ran over. I paid her no mind, though Mater gave her a big hug. I was surprised she hadn't tried to help us sell the shells at the Forum. Mater must have talked her out of it.

"Willem, how much did you sell my shells for? When can I have my money?" she whispered.

Oops! Some businessman I am! I forgot she wasn't included in our plans to leave Rome. I whispered back, "Make me a list of your shells and I'll give you what we sold them for."

95

"Here it is." She pulled out a tablet from the bag she was carrying.

Of course! No one but Elise! I held up my hand, "Give it to me tomorrow."

She frowned and stuck it back in her bag. When we sat down she sat on one side of Mater and I sat on the other. I was hoping she'd sit with her *own* mater!

The service began with Rabbi Saul welcoming everyone. "And tonight I would like to welcome my very dear friends, Serena and Willem. Serena is the owner of the The Cheese Emporium in the next insula west of us. If you've never been there you should try it. She carries some of the best cheese in Rome."

Mater's face flushed, but she was smiling brightly, so I knew it was all right.

Rabbi Saul called on some of the Jewish men to read from the holy scroll he had shown me. I listened carefully. The words spoke of the man Moses making a fiery serpent out of brass, and setting it on a pole. The people had sinned and the Lord God sent fiery serpents among them. But those which were bitten could look at the brass serpent, and they would not die from the snake bites. I wondered at the story. What had the people done that their God would send those serpents after them?

While I was thinking about that, the people sang a song about leaving Babylon and returning to their holy land. Then Rabbi Saul stood and called for Ben to rise and come forward.

"This is Benjamin ben Jacob from our homeland. He is here with his wife, Lanee, and friends, David and Deborah. They have come tonight with a special message from my old friend Yosef, whose father was the greatest rabbi I ever knew. Benjamin ben Jacob and friends, I welcome you to our congregation."

Ben stood alone in front, then he looked at me and motioned for me to come. "I have acquired an interpreter, Willem here. I would like everyone to entirely understand what I say tonight, so I've asked him to come forward. We have never done this before, so please be patient until we are able to get the rhythm of working together."

He stopped, and I told what he'd said in Latin. I saw Mater's eyebrows rise, but then she seemed happy to be able to understand all that was being said, even if she might be worried my knowledge might not be sufficient. She wasn't the only one who thought that!

"My brethren, do you remember in the Torah when our God spoke to Moses out of the burning bush?"

He paused, and I interpreted.

"Do you remember what He said to Moses? Tell them *I AM THAT I AM.*"

Again I spoke it in Latin.

"Tonight our God is speaking the same message to our hearts: *I AM THAT I AM.*"

I told them.

"But tonight He is speaking through the Spirit of His Son that is living in me, *I AM THAT I AM.*"

I interpreted it.

"In the poetry book, the Proverbs of Solomon the son of David, Agur asked, 'what is his name, and what is his son's name, if thou canst tell?'"

I translated it.

"I'm here to answer his question to you, children of Israel.

Tonight I bring a message from the one who said, *I AM THAT I AM*. He says to you, my son's name is Jesus Christ.'

Again I spoke it in Latin.

"Not long ago Jesus Christ lived in our homeland. He went about doing mighty miracles. He took five loaves of bread and two small fishes and fed five thousand men with them! He raised a young girl, a young man, and an older man from the dead. He healed cripples, deaf and dumb people, and even caused some who were blind from birth to see. Thousands heard God speak from heaven one day, saying, *This is my beloved Son, in whom I am well pleased."*

I interpreted each sentence after he spoke it.

"Where is Jesus Christ now? He was tried by the Sanhedrin in Jerusalem, and condemned to die."

I said it in Latin.

"The Romans crucified Him."

I was shocked. I didn't say anything.

Ben looked at me, and said it again. "The Romans crucified Him."

Again I couldn't speak. Someone in the audience interpreted it into Latin.

Ben continued, "But He was the Son of God, and death could not hold Him. After three days He arose from the dead. Over five hundred witnesses saw Him at one time, and verified that He had truly risen from the dead."

I said the Latin words.

"Now, brethren, will you believe on the Son of God? He was raised up on the cross as the serpent was on that pole in the wilderness. Will you look upon Him and believe he died to save you from the sins you have committed against Almighty

God? If you will believe in Him, He will give you eternal life. For He is the only begotten Son of our God, and in Him *is* life! He preached to your brethren in our homeland, *Repent and believe the gospel*—the good news—and you shall be saved."

I interpreted the sentences one by one to many people whose eyes were downcast.

"I bring to you first, the children of Israel, the good news that God will save you from sin to enjoy eternal life through His Son Jesus. Will you believe, repent, and be saved tonight?"

When I finished translating it, I saw that no one was looking at us. Everyone sat quietly looking down at their hands, or at the floor.

Ben waited a long minute for some response then went back to his seat, and I followed him. He sat down beside Lanee, who I saw grip his hand.

I went on back to where Mater sat.

Rabbi Saul came to the front wearing an expression I'd never seen on his face. He looked angry.

"I must express my regret that I have subjected you, my brethren, to this young man's lack of wisdom in addressing you. We have had many claims such as he has spoken of concerning this Jesus Christ person. Would our Messiah be crucified? By the Romans? Benjamin, is this the message that Yosef the son of my Rabbi Ezra would have me to hear from your lips? No, I very much doubt it. Please forgive me, my people. This will not happen again. You are dismissed."

Then he left. I guess he went upstairs, or down to the store.

Without looking at each other, we all left. As I walked home beside Mater, I hated to think of how unhappy Ben and Lanee must be.

CHAPTER ELEVEN

WHAT IS IT, MY HUSBAND?

"BENJAMIN ben Jacob…why don't you come to bed? It is so late," Lanee said sleepily.

He turned from the window's night view of the Forum. "The Lord is giving me a good blessing, Lanee. I don't want to sleep." He brushed his hair back and grinned at her.

"…Philip of Macedonia! That's why you're so happy." Lanee sat up and adjusted the covers. She yawned and said, "In the trouble of what happened tonight, I had forgotten about our talk with him."

"He listened to us, didn't he? And he believed and prayed like a little boy wanting to be saved." Ben came over and grabbed her hand. "How his face shone when he left us! But after our poor reception at the rabbi's tonight, I had just about forgotten the joy of it."

Lanee said, "Then I don't understand."

"Why I'm so happy?"

She studied his dark eyes, and nodded.

"Do you remember when God gave me my love for Jesus?"

Lanee would never forget when Ben had run all the way from his house to Harp's Landing crying out, "Wait, Brother Jonathan, wait for me! Now I can be baptized." God had opened Ben's mourning heart to love Jesus, something he thought he never could do. Ever since then, it seemed to

Lanee that Ben loved the Lord more and more every day.

"He has made me so happy. Even Rabbi Tzadik's opposition before he got saved didn't really take away from my joy. Well, tonight's rejection of our message from Rabbi Saul has given me a true taste of what our Lord went through with the Jewish leaders who didn't believe in Him."

"Yes, love. Rabbi Saul...he doubted you, he dismissed you, and even wished he'd never asked you to speak! Oh, I felt so humiliated, I wanted to pull my shawl over my head and run out of there!"

Ben nodded, "I knew you felt that way, Lanee. And at first I felt like I'd been dealt a punch in my stomach. But as I left the room, I began to see it in a different light. Instead of feeling ashamed and afraid, I got happy! I had followed Jesus into their harsh treatment. I was rejected like He was by them, just this little bit!"

Ben went over to her and placed his strong brown hands on her shoulders. His loving eyes burned into hers. "We both were given the opportunity to endure it for Jesus. Let's give Him thanks right now, Yona. He's so pitiful. He loves us for suffering for Him."

She reached out and pulled him close. "Oh, Ben, I'm beginning to understand. Pray for me that I'll not be ashamed when people doubt and deny Him. Pray for me that I'll feel the same way you do." Lanee's tears flowed down her face. "Oh, Jesus, I'm sorry."

But Ben lifted her face and kissed her cheeks. His lips curved into a beautiful smile as he said, "We are learning so much, aren't we, Yona?"

~~~

"David, you seem so far away tonight," Deborah said. She was resting on the couch next to the window of their palatial room. David was absently looking out the window beside her. He reached down for her hand.

"It was hard tonight when the rabbi rejected Ben's message. It made me remember how it was in Arbela before our rabbi repented and came to Jesus. Though that was on my mind, I've been thinking more about something personal."

"Will you share it with me, my husband?"

David looked down into Deborah's dark eyes. *How beautiful she is!* Her dark hair framed her soft face and curled down over her shoulders. He saw such love in her eyes. David couldn't help but give her a smile. He had found her to be dear to his heart ever since they had married, though before that he knew her rich abba did nothing but spoil her. But a miracle had happened to Deborah when she discovered that both Jesus and David loved her.

He moved away from the window and sat down beside her. In just a moment she was snuggling under his arm.

David said, "My little honeybee, you are my dearest friend—there's nothing about me that I wouldn't like you to know." Then he again grew quiet, staring at the opposite wall of their suite.

"Well?" Deborah reached up and playfully pulled at a curly lock that had fallen over his face.

"I'm trying to think how to tell you about it. I guess I'll just start at the beginning." He turned and faced her. "As you know, my eema and I have been alone since I was born.

My abba is not a Jew. He's a Roman. He was part of the Roman legion stationed in Palestine when Eema was only in her teens.

"They came to our village one day, and my abba saw Eema at the well. He courted and married her, and promised her when he had to leave that he would send for her. By that time she was going to have me. Eema has never heard from him since."

David got up and went back to the window. "Tonight I've been wondering if my abba is somewhere in this city."

After a moment Deborah tilted her head up and asked, "Did your abba know Eema was with child?"

With a frustrated look, David answered, "Eema has never told me that, and I have never asked her. I wouldn't want her to know how much it would hurt me if he did."

Deborah, who was blessed with having both her father and mother raise her, gazed at him tenderly. Then a new thought came to her, and she asked eagerly, "David, did Eema tell you your abba's name?"

"Yes. His name is Marcus Anicia."

"Well, can't we just ask around for him?"

He stood thinking then said, "No, I can't do that, for I have no way of knowing what that would cause." He sat down again beside her and took her hand. Deborah saw a tear begin to travel from the corner of his eye. "Dear girl, will you help me pray for Jesus to lead me to him, and if it is His will, that we meet?"

Deborah reached over and hugged him around the middle. "Oh, yes."

Then she sat back up and said, "David, will you tell me

what your eema would like for you to do? She knew you would want to find him when you came, didn't she?"

"Yes. Before we left, she said, 'Pray for the Lord's will, son.' I know she is praying for us, and for him. I have heard her praying for Jesus to save him many nights."

Deborah wiped the little tear away, leaving her small hand resting on his cheek. She drew his face around to look him in the eyes. "My husband, there is something else I've thought of, and I hope it doesn't hurt you for me to mention it. Do you believe he still lives? After all, he was a soldier. Could it be that he was killed in battle and that is why he never returned?"

"Eema says she is certain he lives. She has assured me that somewhere her husband is alive. It's all I know."

Deborah smiled and said, "Then we will pray and Jesus will lead us to him, if He so wills."

But David didn't smile back. He moved away from her and asked, holding his hands out toward her, "And I, what will I say? What will he say? Will he want to know me?" He bowed his head between his hands and worried, "Will he be glad to meet me? Or will he be ashamed of me?"

Deborah rose up and then knelt beside his knees, "Let's pray now, David, and give it into Jesus' hands."

David slowly got up and knelt down beside her. With his head on his arms, he started thinking of the life he and Eema had lived before he'd met Jesus—how lonely and poor they were. Jesus had given him such a blessed new life: Lanee and her family, the Holy Ghost filling him on the day of Pentecost, good jobs and a new home in Arbela. He'd even sent him Deborah to share his life. He remembered his love for Jesus then, and his tears really came. After he wept, he was able to pray, "Jesus, I trust you with my abba."

CHAPTER TWELVE

PREACHING IN THE FORUM

Ben and Lanee showed up at our insula early. They must have been the first to come through the door of the cheese shop. I guess they told Mater about my new job, for she sent Ben up to get me.

"Willem, wake up! Willem! We need you this morning!"

When I peeked out of eyelids barely slit, all I could see were two burning eyes under a curly brush of dark hair. He was leaning over my cot.

"Oh...it's you, Ben. Wait...wait a minute. Let me get ready."

"I'll go back downstairs and try some of your eema's cheese. See you soon!"

I closed my eyes again. It was something I never expected— Ben waking me up this morning. And something else was wrong. Where did he get that excited smile he gave me as he left for downstairs? The mystery caused me to jump up. *Last night Rabbi Saul really lashed him with his tongue. I thought he'd be ashamed or mad. What happened?*

As soon as I pounded down the stairs, Ben and Lanee thanked Mater, and we left for the Forum.

"David and Deborah are meeting us there. I want to speak when the first shoppers get there," Ben said as we raced down the street.

"Are you sure, Ben? If Rabbi Saul didn't believe you

last night…"

"Willem, don't worry about that. I'm here to tell people the good news. I know everyone will not believe me. Will you help me?"

"Well, I'm not sure *I* believe you. Does that matter?"

"No, if you'll promise to translate what I say as well as you're able. I will pay you for it, and as we go along you can decide what you believe. There's only one thing you should know, Willem—if they get mad at me, you'll probably get blamed too."

"What do you think will happen?"

"I don't know for sure. They crucified Jesus."

I thought about that as we hurried on. I knew the emperor and the army could arrest and even execute anyone who displeased them, but I couldn't see that happening to Ben and Lanee.

"I'm willing to give it a try. Maybe we Romans will treat you better than your Jews did Jesus."

When we reached the Forum, David and Deborah were waiting for us.

"Good morning, friends," Lanee said. "Here's some breakfast. Willem's eema sells delicious cheese in her shop. She wants us to stop by when we're finished here."

David and Deborah sat on a nearby bench and dug into the bread and cheese Mater had sent.

I sat down beside them and said, "I love your singing, David. And I like the way you strum the harp along with it."

David munched and said between bites, "The day we left Arbela, our friend Yosef pressed his old harp into my hand. He said, 'My abba's instrument needs some hand oil on it.' I learned to play the chords as we sailed here. Then I met Anthony, one of the sailors on Benjamin's Dove who could speak Latin, so I asked him to help me translate some of my songs."

He finished his breakfast, brushed off his hands, and said, "What's our plan, Brother Ben?"

Ben said, "Will you and Deborah sing that song you were singing on the ship first? I remember it said 'Jesus loves you' in Latin. Maybe it will at least inspire curiosity about Jesus—who might this be that loves me?"

David picked up the harp and took Deborah's hand. "Are you ready my fair one, to sing our first duet in this amazing city?"

Deborah smiled beautifully, and said, "I'll try to help you, though I know your eema would do a better job."

David said, "Not today. You will win every heart with your smile, sweet wife."

We followed them into the Forum, and Ben motioned us to the stairs of Julius Caesar's temple.

We climbed the stairs then the rest of us stepped back. Deborah and David stood alone at the top of the stairs. They were two of the most beautiful people I had ever seen. He could have been one of our Roman gods, and she a goddess. They wore simple flowing tunics—David's was girded by a leather belt and Deborah's had a girdle all covered with fancy stitches. His hair was curling around his ears and his face was covered in an equally curly beard. Her long black hair matched his, all curly and wavy, falling below the waist of her tunic. I held my breath waiting for their first notes, wondering how they would be received by the crowds of

Romans already here this morning.

David struck a chord on the harp then began to sing:

"Oh, how sweet the moment,
When first I realized,
That Jesus Christ the Savior,
Would look into my eyes,
That I could mean something
 To one so great and pure,
I found out the blessed truth,
There's not a doubt,
That Jesus loves me!"

Then Deborah joined him in harmony:

"Oh, now I know that Jesus loves me!
The Son of God in heaven loves me!
I am completely sure that Jesus loves me!
He brought me out and saved my soul,
Yes, Jesus loves me!"

The people were all still and quiet, so David sang the whole song over again, and he and Deborah sang the chorus together two more times.

That's when Ben stepped out two stairs down and began his message.

"God sent His only begotten Son to us. He brought to us the good news that we don't have to perish for our sins!"

I stepped down with him, cleared my throat, and interpreted his words into my best Latin. My voice didn't sound deep and mature as Ben's did. It was squeaky, and I'm sure I sounded scared.

"Every one of us has sinned! But Jesus Christ, the sinless Son of God, carried our sins to the cross and died, so we don't have to suffer for them."

Again my voice obeyed though my knees were shaking.

"We can be set free from sin, if we will repent and believe in Jesus!"

I said it in Latin, looking at the faces of the people as I spoke. They were beginning to look surprised at the message.

"God sent us to Rome to tell you the good news that you might believe and be saved!"

I interpreted the last sentence and waited for more.

Suddenly Ben motioned to David and Deborah and they again sang their sweet song. Ben grabbed my hand and we descended to the paving stones of the Forum. Lanee joined us.

The people listened again. Then as the last note died away, I expected the crowd would return to their shopping as if nothing had happened. But, to my surprise, they began to gather around us.

A man called out, "Where have you come from? How do you know these things you've told us today?" Another said, "Why do you speak to us of sin? What are the sins you're talking about?"

Ben and Lanee both looked at me hoping I'd tell them what they were saying. How could I interpret all these questions? The people went on asking, and each question led to another and another!

"Ben, Lanee, they're asking too many questions. They want to know where you're from, and how do you know what you've said is true. They want to know about sin and still they're asking more questions!"

"Tell them we'll be back tomorrow and answer their questions one by one. Tell them to come early again, and we will be here to talk to them about Jesus Christ."

I told the crowd what he said. The circle began to break up. I saw Ben and Lanee smiling at the people, and David and Deborah both nodding their heads to the men and women who looked them over as they walked away.

As we left the Forum, I looked back and saw many of the people watching us leave. I could tell they were thinking about the song and what Ben had said. All my life in Rome, I'd never seen that particular expression on Roman faces. It was rapt interest. I was amazed!

We headed across town to Mater's cheese shop. Everyone was quiet, until Lanee spoke.

"Willem, I need an interpreter. I need to be able to talk to the girls and women. Do you know someone who would help me?"

I did. *Elise.*

But I didn't want to get her.

First of all, she is a brat.

I didn't say a word.

"Did you hear me, Willem? Did you understand what I said?"

Secondly, I don't like her. She's pushy.

Lanee looked at Ben and shrugged.

"Willem?" This time Ben was talking. "You don't know anyone that could help Lanee interpret tomorrow?"

Thirdly, she isn't a boy, but a grubby little girl.

It must have been the sour look I felt my face wearing that made them all call me at once, "Willem!"

"What?" I said hoping they'd drop the subject when they saw I didn't have an answer. But they all stopped and were waiting. "All right, I do know someone. But I have to warn you, she's a naughty little girl, who is pushy and messy. And I don't like her a bit!"

They all burst out laughing. Then Lanee said, "Lead me to her...this I have to see!"

I said, "Let's talk to Mater about it first. She may have a better suggestion."

But when we reached the cheese shop and told Mater, guess who she suggested? I told Lanee where to find her. I had no desire to hunt her up.

While she was busy with that, Ben wanted to know every question the crowd in the Forum had asked us. I loaned him a wax tablet and stylus, and he made a list of what they wanted to know. He said, "I will be ready tomorrow."

When Lanee came back, she looked really amused. She said, "Elise will meet us here in the morning. She told her eema not to worry about her, for she would be with Willem."

I knew it. It had already started.

When our four friends left, Mater asked me to watch the store for her. I was past hungry so I cut me a nice slice of our best smoked cheese. As I munched on it I wandered out in front of the store just to see who might pass by.

Across the street I noticed a soldier. He was tall, with strong legs and muscled arms. He took off his helmet and I was surprised to see that he was bald on top. Not many young Romans are bald. *He must be older than most soldiers,* I thought. He was buying some almonds from Portent's store. When he turned around I saw several round silver and gold badges hanging on his belts. He threw some of the roasted nuts into his mouth. Then he turned back and nodded and paid for them. I watched him turn from the counter and look in my direction.

I suddenly dropped my eyes. I heard the jangling of his belts and the hard chuffing sound coming from the hob-nails meeting the pavement.

I only saw the rugged sandals stop in front of me. "May I examine your cheeses, son?" he said.

I raised my head and looked into his clear blue eyes. "Yes, Pater."

CHAPTER THIRTEEN

PATER'S SON

A T first we just looked at each other. Then I saw something start up in my father's blue eyes. He must have known I was his son all along, yet it pleased him that I knew *him*. Soon I saw his lips curving into the first smile I ever saw on his face. It was so beautiful—straight white teeth and an excited expression in his eyes. I liked him!

Something else new happened...suddenly I felt *taken care of.*

"Want to show me your cheese now, son?"

He followed me into our shop. I was so excited. I didn't know what to do first. Of course, I needed to call Mater. But I wanted to just be with him alone for maybe another minute or so.

"Pater? Shall I call Mater to come?" I asked.

He quit looking around the shop and gave his attention to me. "Will you first come here?"

I obeyed, walking up as close to his soldier's uniform as I dared. He laid his helmet and package of almonds down on the counter. Then he opened his arms, pulled me to him, and hugged me hard. Surely he felt my heart about to beat out of my chest. When he let go of the squeeze, I got my arms around him and lay my head on his decorated chest and hugged—and cried, "Pater, Pater, I have missed you. I have missed you."

When I looked up into his eyes, they were full of tears.

"I will be here for you, son. I will need to take care of some things first...then I will be here for you."

I let go, and called out, "Mater! Mater! Please come quickly!"

"What is it, Willem? I'm not finished with our supper yet," she answered a little impatiently.

Pater called out, "I hope it is your excellent roast pork and squash!"

Then he did something amazing. Without a bit of warning he dashed up the stairs faster than even Leo could have. I was left with my mouth hanging open.

It was all quiet. I didn't know whether to follow him or wait. I decided to wait. I began to close up the shop. Even though it was early, we were not going to tend to it anymore today. Pater was home!

When I finished everything, I called, "Is supper ready? The shop is closed."

Pater came down the stairs to get me. I picked up his helmet and almonds and went upstairs with him.

"Mater!" I cried out when I saw her. She looked so happy. The worry lines were gone. Her mouth curved up into a sweet smile.

"How did you know he was your pater, Willem? We both were trying to guess." Mater took hold of Pater's hand.

"It is his broad shoulders. They are built just like mine. He stands like I do too. He had to be my pater." I moved over near him, and he draped his other arm around my neck.

Can you stay for supper, Pater? We have missed you so. Can you stay awhile? I thought these words, but I didn't speak them. I remembered Mater's word *hindrance.* I also remembered my vow not to be one, but to be a help to my pater.

Pater said, "I have time to eat with you, tonight, but then I must return to the camp. But I will try to come back and see you tomorrow afternoon."

We ate together, talking all the time about the years we'd missed. Mater told him how well the cheese shop was doing, and I told him about my knack for learning and speaking other languages. He told us that he thought he would be one of the Praetorian Guard helping to guard the palace, though the emperor lived in Capri, not Rome.

"Didn't Tiberius come to Rome when you came, Pater?"

"So, it *was* you I saw on the corbita!"

"Yes! Mater, didn't I tell you?"

"I saw your mother's hair, and knew it was my Serena, and saw my big boy beside her! But the distance was great and I wanted to see you so badly, I thought, oh it couldn't be. But, it was!"

"Pater, I love you."

"I love you, too, son."

I knew after we ate that Mater wanted time to be with Pater, and I needed to take the abalone shells to Nicholas. I told my pater about them. He knew who Nicholas was.

"Son, I will go back to the camp soon. No one knows that I have you and Mater, but I will be there if you need me. I am in the second row of buildings on the left from the gate, in the third one. Look for it when you go in today. I have displayed a red cloth on the door in preparation for letting you know where to find me any time. I am your pater, and from this day I will be your protector."

"Thank you, Pater."

I gave him another hug then I lifted my bag of shells and left for the camp.

I headed out toward the eastern edge of Rome. My frats and I had explored the outside of the camp but I'd never before had a reason to go inside it. What an opportunity!

The whole of the Praetorian Camp was surrounded by a deep ditch, then a high wall. I went to the front gate and asked for Nicholas. The guard directed me to the main building ahead. It was full of soldiers coming and going. They were mostly just dressed in their off-white tunics and boots.

I asked one of them where I could find Nicholas the steward. He pointed out a large table toward the back. When I walked up with my bag, Nicholas saw me and motioned me to sit down. I sat on a stool nearby, and watched the busy goings-on as I waited.

When Nicholas finished with the soldier, he came over to me. "Greetings, Willem. I'm glad you came. Follow me to my quarters, where we can talk."

We left through the back door of the long building and then around to the front, but before we went on, Nicholas had to cough. I remembered what Pater had said and as we passed the second row of buildings I caught sight of a red cloth on the door of the third one down.

We went on past all those barracks to some smaller buildings along the wall. Nicholas led me to his, unlocked the door, and motioned for me to enter. When my eyes adjusted to the shade inside, I was startled. I don't know *what* I expected, but this wasn't it. The whole room was how I imagined the rooms of the emperor's palace to look. I turned from its splendor and stared at Nicholas.

"Do you like it, Willem?"

"It is grand! But…"

Nicholas coughed into his arm then said, "Sit down, son, I know you've had a long walk. I'll get you some juice."

He passed through a rich black curtain and came back in a few minutes with some grape juice. I accepted the cup. It looked like a silver one. I really don't know, for I had never experienced holding one. I drank some of the juice then let my eyes travel over the many things I'd never seen before displayed in that room.

"I wanted you to see my home, Willem. I don't ever invite any of the soldiers here, and I have had a desire for someone to see it lately. It is my hideaway. Out there I am the buyer, seller, and distributor of what equipment and food the soldiers need to serve. In here I am the emperor in my palace.

"I have acquired some of the finest booty that was ever carried off from the many lands my soldiers have visited. I doubt even the emperor himself has one of these fine chairs made of ivory and ebony. And have you ever seen a rug like this, Willem? It is the fur of a tiger from as far east and north as the whole earth goes."

"I have never seen anything like any of this before, sir."

After he coughed again, he said, "May I see the abalone shells you brought me?"

I took the sack over to where he sat, hoping that none of the sand would dirty his floor. He began to pull them out one by one, admiring their shiny smooth insides. The largest one he laid aside from the others. When all twenty lay on the table, he said, "I will give you ten denarii for these," motioning to all the others, "but for this one I will give you twenty denarii for it alone."

"I...don't understand."

"I know what I am doing, and the value of this one is great. I do not want to cheat you, Willem."

"Yes, sir."

He coughed into his sleeve and said, "Will you be making any more shell-gathering trips?" He walked over to an ornately carved wooden box and began counting silver coins out of it.

"I think so."

When he counted out the money to me, I placed it in the bottom of the empty sack and tied it up so it wouldn't jingle.

"Again, I will take all you can find for ten denarii apiece, and if you find another exceptionally large one, I will give you much more for it. Now I must return to work. I will see you to the gate, son."

He stood up and immediately had a coughing spat. When it subsided, we walked out into the afternoon sunshine toward the gate.

"Thank you, Willem," he said and left me at the gate.

Two-hundred and ten denarii! I walked through the gate, stuffed the money sack down the front of my tunic then set to running across Rome. *Leo, Senny, Blue, Turk—look what I've got!*

CHAPTER FOURTEEN

PATER

LUCIUS Dio had a hard time sleeping that night back at camp.

Willem is big for his age! He's bright, too! Pater smiled as he remembered Willem recognizing him. *But, yes, he does have my shoulders, though I think he'll end up taller than I am. Serena is still so beautiful. I'll never forget the look on her face when I ran up those stairs.*

She objected to my so openly coming to see them…said I could jeopardize my army career! I told her I'd had enough of being away from her and Willem, and didn't care what it cost me. I think she's happy…oh, yes, I know she's happy!

She is having a hard time keeping Willem home. That's just how I was…and that's why I am in the army. But I've had enough of seeing what the world is like…I want to know what my son is like, and I want to enjoy my sweet Serena's company.

The bunk was much better than many he'd slept in, yet he couldn't doze off. His mind went back to his return to Rome, and how his commander had pulled strings to get him his new position. He had always done his best to be a good Roman soldier. He had fought in battles that had won him many badges of honor. Then his general had tapped him to be his administrative assistant. He didn't even know he had a talent for such work, but in no time he had become almost indispensible to his commander.

And when he knew my time was short, he surprised me by

121

sending me to Rome. And just tonight I learned I will head the police force here. Pater mused about what kind of life he would be living a year from now. He'd be able to marry Serena openly and claim his son. He'd help her in the cheese shop and maybe even open another one somewhere else in Rome.

What would Willem like to do? It made him sad to realize how little he knew about Willem.

The barracks Pater slept in held seventy-nine other soldiers. When his promotion came, he would be moved into the centurion's quarters at the end of the barracks. He was used to living with other soldiers in the field, in tents, but lately he'd been quartered in the stone buildings of the Roman forts.

After going over and over the thrilling reunion with his family, he knew he needed to fall asleep. Buzzing, whistling, and sawing snores filled the darkened room. Pater closed his eyes and tried to ignore the fracas.

Another sound caught his attention. It was soft and low, but it was a voice speaking. Pater listened. It sounded as if it were coming from the bunk against the other wall. Pater shifted his frame toward the sound and waited.

"…Will you make yourself known to me? I know you are real. I have read about you and I would like to hear your voice…just once. Oh, please let me…Lord."

The voice stopped and waited. Pater waited, too. He trained his eyes across the aisle hoping to locate the right bunk the next time the voice spoke.

"Just once, Lord." The voice had changed into a husky whisper. Pater thought he detected tears in the words.

"Just tonight, Lord…I need your help…my wife is so far

away. So many years I've left her alone. How I wish I could see her again. I don't even know if she's still alive! She was one of yours, Lord—so young and sweet. I was so wrong to leave her like I did."

Someone coughed, and Pater saw a man in the bunk across the aisle jump. The snores were all he heard after that.

Who was he talking to? Maybe Jupiter or Apollo? Surely he wasn't expecting one of the gods to help him find his wife.

Pater gave up trying to fall asleep after that. His eyes had briefly closed as dawn crept into the room. But then the trumpet sounded, ending any hope of his nap. He lay still and watched the bunk across the room. Soon a grizzled man arose from it and stretched. He was close to Pater's age and in much need of having his hair and beard barbered. He scanned the whole room as he flexed his muscled arms. Pater let his eyes drop shut.

He's afraid someone has heard his prayer, Pater thought. He remembered how in the heat of battle he himself had thrown out prayers to the gods when survival seemed too desperate to hope for.

The god the legionnaire prayed to was called "the Lord." Pater had never heard of that one.

A voice from the back of the room called out, "Marcus, hold up, and I'll go with you to the bath." Pater saw a younger soldier waving his hand. The man nodded sleepily and sat back down on his bunk. He reached under it and pulled out some clothes. Then he waited with his head in his hands. Soon his friend came up and they both went out the door.

Not really considering why, Pater rose up, grabbed some clean clothes, and followed them.

CHAPTER FIFTEEN

THE CROWD AT
THE FORUM

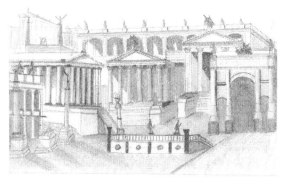

Ben came to get me again early the next morning. The first thing I did was tell him about my pater, a decorated Roman soldier! Then I remembered how telling others could make me a hindrance. *I have to remember not to tell anyone else.*

We met David and Deborah near the marble Julius Caesar, and soon Lanee showed up with Elise.

Ben said, "I promised to answer their questions today. Should I do it in the big group, or should we split up and work separately?" He brushed back the hair that fell over his brow. I liked the excited look he had in his dark eyes.

Boldly I said, "Yesterday they kept asking more and more questions. Maybe start out by answering those questions."

"That sounds good, Willem. David, you and Deborah

125

get their attention with another song. Then Willem and I'll take over."

David strummed the harp and the two of them sang a song that said, "I'm so glad that Jesus saved me!" After the first sounds of their voices, I was amazed to see people running toward us from the other end of the Forum. Maters pulled their little ones along, slaves grabbed up their shopping bags and headed our way, businessmen and even some who looked like the nobility of Rome came quickly toward us so they could hear the song.

David and Deborah gave them plenty of time by singing the song over and over, especially those words, "I'm so glad, yes, so thankful and glad, that Jesus saved me!"

Ben and I stepped out and he began to speak, "You asked me many questions after I preached yesterday. I promised I would answer them one by one today. So I will begin."

As I translated, I saw others coming from the streets that led to the Forum.

"I am Benjamin ben Jacob, and this is my wife Lanee." He held out his arm to her, and she came, smiling.

I translated it, and waited.

"The two who sang the beautiful song are David ben Lira and his wife Deborah. We are all from Palestine. We have come here to witness to you of the visitation we have had from God Almighty. He is Lord of Heaven and Earth."

I tried to translate it. How should I say "God Almighty" in Latin? I had never heard it spoken before. I finally said *the all-powerful God.*

"He sent His Son to our world and specifically to Palestine about 34 years ago. He came in the form of a newborn baby.

The baby was born of a virgin."

When I said it in Latin, the people seemed to suck in the words like they were the air they were breathing. Their eyes went from Ben to me and back again, as if they were feasting on every word. As for me, I found that I also was excited to hear what he'd say next.

"He was named of the holy angel who visited the virgin. The angel said, 'He shall be called Jesus.'"

Again their eyes left Ben and turned on me as I gave the interpretation. How could I translate *angel,* and what are angels? I just used the Hebrew word.

"Jesus grew up and began to preach to the people in Palestine. He said that He was the Son of God, and wanted to teach them of His Father, God Almighty."

I translated.

"Jesus was a man who went about doing good. He healed lepers, blind men, the crippled, and sick. He even raised three dead people to life again. He fed multitudes with a few fishes and small loaves of bread."

As I spoke the Latin words, I felt proud to speak them. But, why?

Ben said, "Though He was such a blessing to all of us in that land, the religious leaders did not believe in Him. They arrested Him, and accused Him before Pontius Pilate, the Roman governor, and finally convinced him to crucify Jesus."

When I translated this, a gasp rose from the crowd.

"They placed His body in a tomb and sealed the tomb, even placing soldiers before it to guard it."

I told them.

"But on the third day, Jesus arose from the dead! Over

five hundred people saw Him at once, alive again!"

I spoke the Latin words, and the crowd clapped and cheered.

"For forty days He was among us showing Himself alive by many proofs, then He was taken up in a cloud back to His Father in Heaven. And that's where He is right now!"

When I translated it, it seemed they were disappointed to hear He was gone.

"But Jesus promised when He left, that He would send the Spirit of God from Heaven. He called Him another Comforter, the Holy Ghost. And ten days later a group of believers in Jesus were together in an upper room in Jerusalem, and this Comforter, the Spirit of truth, came to them."

I translated it.

"The Holy Ghost filled every one of them and they all spoke in a language they did not know. Tongues of fire sat on their heads, and when one of Jesus' followers preached that day, three thousand souls believed and were saved."

I told it in Latin, feeling amazed.

"I have received the Holy Ghost, and that is why I have come to tell you these things, that you also may believe and be saved!"

I translated these words, and then Ben said, "I will now step down to the pavement and answer your other questions, with Willem's help. My wife will answer the women's questions with her interpreter Elise's help. Thank you for your kind attention."

I told them, and we went down among them.

"What does it mean to be saved?" "Is God Almighty the only real God?" "What must I do to be saved?" "What is sin?"

"What if I am not saved, what will happen?"

So many questions, hard questions! But each time Ben gave the answer, and we learned things that we'd never heard before. Lanee was busy with the women and Elise was holding her own. I heard her little piping voice working hard to help Lanee explain her answers to the women who couldn't understand her foreign tongue.

David and Deborah strolled down the Forum and soon were singing another song. Listening to them, I lost track for a moment with Ben. It was beautiful. They sang, "Jesus, the One who loves me so…"

Jesus…would Jesus have loved me? Oh, if only I could have met Him.

What seemed like a hundred questions later, we left for home. Ben and everyone else dropped Elise and me off at our insulas, and I set out to find my fraters.

They were lounging on Senny's steps. But they all sat up when I told them what I'd been doing. Leo let out a low whistle and said, "I knew you were brave, Bo, but did you actually talk to all those high and mighties in the Forum?"

"Yes, and I want you to be there tomorrow. I want all of you to hear Ben and the rest. They're paying me ten denarii a day to translate for them!"

They all let out a happy whoop when they heard that.

Senny said, "Does anyone listen?"

I said, "Come and see!"

"What is Ben saying?" Turk asked.

"Remember on the boat, when they acted so crazy and were crying out, 'Thank you, Jesus!'? They're telling about Him. You should have seen the people come running yesterday as soon as David and Deborah started to sing! Even some of the nobility showed up!"

Blue looked a little troubled. He said, "Jesus is not another god, is He, Willem? We've got enough of them in Rome already!"

I answered, "He doesn't seem to be like all of *them*, Blue. Just come and hear Ben, and then you can decide."

They all promised to see me in the morning, and I left for the cheese shop.

Pater was there! He was sitting in the back room having a cool drink with Mater. When I walked in, he got up and hugged me. I liked the way he smelled, clean and leathery. He kept his arm around me as we walked back where Mater was sitting.

"Mater tells me you have a translating job at the Forum."

"Yes, sir. This is my second day there. Would you like to meet Ben and Lanee, and their friends, David and Deborah?"

"I would. Where did you meet them?"

"The day we saw you on the barge, we were going to the Great Sea to gather shells. On the way back, we hired passage on a ship from Palestine. We met them there." I looked at Mater. She smiled up at me, and I knew all of it was in her mind too—the sea, the shells, the ride home on the ship, and the crazy young couples rejoicing around us!

"What are they doing in the Forum that they need you to translate?"

"They are singing and telling anyone who will listen about Jesus."

Pater's face changed a little. "Who is Jesus?"

"I am only beginning to learn who He is, though I heard

about Him one day here in the shop. He is a man that lived in Palestine and was a miracle worker. He was crucified, Pater! But Ben said He rose again!"

"So Ben is preaching a new god in the Forum?"

"Yes, sir. He is."

"And you are helping him by translating his words?"

"Yes, sir."

"Willem, I haven't had any time to know what you believe about the gods, and I'm not sure what I myself believe about them, but I know that Rome is very religious and sometimes jealous for their gods. I think I'd better come and listen to what Ben says tomorrow. Will you be there then?"

"I believe so. Ben will come for me early in the morning."

"You will see me there. Now let's have some lunch, if you are ready, Serena."

Mater touched his hand as she rose to get the food from the counter beside the table.

"When are you on duty again, my love?" she asked. My tired old mother had flown away somewhere. In her place was someone with soft and happy eyes.

A customer came to buy some cheese, so I stepped to the front to help her. It was Elise's mother. She peered past the counter to where Mater and Pater sat.

"Good day, Serena! I needed a little cheese to go with the brown bread I bought at the market just now. How is everyone?"

Mater called back, "We are well and happy. Willem will help you with your cheese, Dorcas. Lucius, this is my friend who lives in the next insula. She has a daughter who is one of Willem's friends."

I slightly shook my head. Pater saw me then he smiled back at her. "I'm glad to meet you."

I sliced the cheese she'd handed me. I noticed how she had the same big brown eyes that Elise had, though she wasn't at all skinny.

She said, "Elise was so glad you took her with you and helped her make some money from the shells. She is anxious to go back. Do you think you will go any time soon?"

"Uh...I don't know. I have another job."

"Oh, yes, and so does she! But it doesn't seem that your new jobs will last too long. Well, I must be going! Good-bye, you two," she called out to Mater and Pater as she left.

Elise! She was helping Lanee explain left and right today. She's a smart little girl, even if she is spoiled.

After she left, we ate our meal. Pater asked if I would watch the cheese shop long enough for Mater and him to be alone to talk upstairs. They took the dishes upstairs, and I settled down to wait for customers.

The next morning Ben came early. I was already up and dressed feeling excited about Pater coming today. *What will he think?*

We joined Lanee and Elise coming from her place. The morning in Rome seemed just like any other. The shops were beginning to open. Some little children were playing on their steps. As I walked by Leo's, he stuck his head out the window, and soon I heard his fast steps catching up. I didn't know exactly when Turk, Blue, and Senny joined us. Now they followed us down the street to the Via Sacra, and into the Forum. Some people were already gathered together near Caesar's statue. When they saw us, they cheered. David and

Deborah joined us then. We went up the steps of the temple.

I listened with my eyes on the crowd as David and Deborah sang their song. It was the one that says, "And now I know Jesus loves me..." The crowd grew as they sang.

When David and Deborah went down the stairs, they stood near Lanee at the edge of the crowd. I was beside Ben at the top of the stairs ready to begin interpreting what he spoke. That's when I saw two soldiers joining the crowd. One was a lean, tall man. The other was my pater.

I was amazed to see how great a crowd was gathering. The pavement was full, and many were sitting on the steps of the nearby temple. My fraters had joined them. I gave them a big proud grin.

Ben began. "I see the Lord has sent you again to hear His Word, and many new ones are here. Welcome!"

I translated it and tried smiling out at the crowd just as Ben did.

"I have come today to tell you that Jesus Christ is the Son of the *living* God. He is our creator. The Lord God made the earth and everything in it, including us!"

I said the words in Latin, and I saw a frown cross my pater's face.

"When He sent His Son into the world a little more than three decades ago, it was because He loved His creation, and wanted to save us from our sins. If you will believe in His Son Jesus Christ, He will take His Son's precious blood that was shed on the cross, and wash all your sins away. He will save you!"

I translated the words. I noticed the tall soldier who came with Pater seemed very interested in what Ben was saying.

"Today if you are hungry to know God and His Son Jesus, I will ask you to kneel on the pavement. When you kneel, begin to talk to God your own way. His ear is open to your prayer. He will hear you. He will forgive you. He will save you, for His Son has made the way. His Son *is* the way!"

I poured the words out just as Ben had said them, letting my voice match the fervency of his. Suddenly it seemed the whole crowd fell to their knees. And just as suddenly, they were praying. I looked at Ben and saw his dark eyes were amazed. He hurried down the steps and I followed him.

I saw the tall soldier beside my pater had knelt, but Pater had not.

Ben and Lanee moved through the kneeling ones, laying their hands on their heads, and praying to God in Jesus' name. I translated Ben's prayer, and Elise translated Lanee's. David and Deborah began their song at the top of the steps.

I felt a hand on my arm, and looked up. It was Pater. He motioned for me to come with him. Ben looked up, and I mouthed, *my pater.* He nodded.

I caught my fraters' eyes as I followed my father's hob-nailed sandals out of the crowd and out of the Forum. Turk drew his hand in a cutting motion over his throat. I knew he wasn't being funny.

Chapter Sixteen

Do You Believe in Jesus, Willem?

"SON, let's walk a little before we talk. I need to think about what I've heard before I know what to tell you."

"I usually help Ben until it's all over, Pater."

"He saw me, and was willing for me to take you with me, Willem."

We turned south taking the Via Appia. He was leading me at a fast pace. Suddenly I realized why. *I am his son. He is not supposed to be my pater. Oh, no. I am being a hindrance!*

We marched out of town and down the grave-lined road. His face was also grave. Finally he turned aside to a wooded area behind that life-sized marble statue of a soldier on a horse. I followed and stopped when he did. At a marble bench between two graves he motioned me to sit down.

He sat and faced me.

"Do you realize what trouble you could make for our family by doing what you did back there, Willem?" Pater's blue eyes bore into mine. Then he looked away. When he turned back to me, he said, "No, let me start again. First of all, do you believe the words you were speaking today?"

I couldn't answer him. So I just smiled at him. Pater and I were together, whatever the reason, and I was glad!

"Wait, son. I know you are only eleven years old. I know you don't understand how cruel Rome can be. Also I know that I haven't been here to teach you anything. But, Willem, do you trust me?"

"I...I believe in you, Pater." I smiled again.

Pater didn't smile back. "Then why do you stand in the Forum crying out words that could cause our whole family to be crucified, too?" He stood up, looking worried.

I stood up and said, "Why? We are not breaking the law, are we? I have heard many speakers in the Forum before."

"Have you ever seen people kneeling and praying before?"

"No, sir. Wasn't that amazing?"

"Yes, it was." He lowered his voice and glanced back toward the road. "But it was also dangerous. If Tiberius were to hear of it, or if a Senator took offense, you could be in deep trouble. And *I* may be the one who would have to arrest you!"

"You arrest me?"

"Yes, I have just been appointed one of the centurions in charge of keeping peace in the city. My job is to arrest those who disturb the peace."

Pater's face suddenly lost its tenseness, He sat back down, and when I sat down, I saw his worried expression had melted. "Son, you're a great interpreter. You did a powerful job! But I must ask you not to do it another time."

Looking into his blue eyes, I remembered the longing I'd felt just to meet him. Now I could see he loved me. It was worry he felt and not really anger. I said, "Then what shall Ben do? He's counting on me to interpret for him. And I'm being paid ten denarii every day I translate."

"Do you know Ben's plans?" he asked.

"I don't."

"Perhaps you and I should talk to Ben this evening."

"Yes...yes, sir. I know where they are staying."

"I will come for you and we will go there."

We walked almost back to the city together then split up. He headed to camp, and I went home. When I got there Mater looked up from trimming a cheese, surprised to see me.

"Already done?"

"Pater came. He took me away before it was over."

"Oh?"

"He's afraid we may get in trouble."

"What? Why would Pater think that?"

"Today a great crowd gathered to hear Ben, and when he finished most of the people knelt on the pavement and prayed. When that happened, Pater came and took me with him. He is coming this evening so we can meet with Ben. He wants to know what his plans are about preaching in the Forum."

Mater had quit trimming. Looking shocked, she said, "Willem, you must do whatever your pater tells you to do. He knows the authorities."

"I will do as he says, Mater. I believe he will decide after we meet Ben tonight."

We both got lost in our own thoughts then, I guess. Mater was worried, I could see. She bent her head over the chopping board, drawing the knife slowly through the hardened cheeses.

Just then I heard Senny's whistle outside the shop. Mater heard it, too, and nodded that I could go. I followed Senny over to Leo's stoop.

"What happened, Willem?" Turk asked. They were all draped over Leo's steps.

"Were you arrested?" Blue said.

"Please don't tell anyone, frats, but he was my pater."

I knew they were surprised. I'd never had a pater before. "No, he didn't arrest me, but he was upset. He has forbidden me to interpret for Ben in the Forum again."

Then I said, "Did you like it?"

Senny said, "It made me want to get to meet Jesus. But why is Ben preaching about someone who is dead?"

"Didn't you hear him say He arose?"

"Yes, I heard him say it, but I'm not sure I believe it. People who die don't rise up," Senny replied.

I came back, "If Jesus *is* the Son of God, He can do anything, right?"

Blue put in, "Sure He *could*. But all the gods claim to do such things."

"But, Blue, somehow Jesus is different," I said, remembering the feeling I had when Ben told about how they crucified Jesus.

Blue answered, "I heard him, but I don't want a god, not even a nice one."

Turk put his arm around his brother's neck, and they both stared down at the step. I waited for Blue to explain, but he didn't say another word.

Leo pulled on the sleeve of my tunic. "So, do you believe in Jesus, Bo?"

"Lanee said Jesus showed me to her before she came to Rome. That's why she and the other three were dancing around us in the boat. Jesus is so amazing; the more I hear about Him, the more I want to hear!"

I thought about Blue and Turk as I walked back to the

shop. I really didn't know much about their family. I thought, because they had household gods, they must be believers in them. I'd learned today that Blue didn't...anymore.

Back inside the shop, as I swept up I wondered if I would be interpreting for Ben again. It didn't seem likely. I remembered the pavement of the Forum covered with kneeling Romans. It was a scene I never expected to see in my lifetime. Romans did not kneel, except to the emperor.

But then I remembered Ben's message.

Oh, Jesus. How I wish I could know Him. I wish He would've come here to Rome.

Jesus...do you love ME? I was surprised at myself and at how my words were directed up as if I were speaking to a really tall person. Well...I might as well go ahead and ask Him...didn't Ben say He is alive above in Heaven? Maybe He can hear me...*Jesus, do you hear me? If you do, will you help my pater to agree for me to help Ben in the Forum again? I want to learn more of you, and I want my pater to learn of you too. So Jesus, cause Pater to change his mind, at least about tomorrow.*

I waited hoping to get an answer, but there was nothing. Yet I felt like my words were received. Talking to the marble gods hadn't felt like this. It was almost as if a real invisible ear were turned in my direction.

When Pater came for me it was getting dark. I had worked in the shop for Mater, and between customers the whole afternoon I kept thinking of what Ben had preached about Jesus. Most of all I thought about His dying on the cross.

I had never seen anyone crucified, though I knew it was our way of executing criminals. When Pater showed up, and as we walked the streets to the Lex Roma, I asked, "Pater, have you ever seen anyone crucified?"

"Yes." Pater didn't slow down or say any more.

I hurried along with him down the crowded street and as we turned the corner to the Forum, I said, "Will you tell me about it?"

"I would rather not."

By then we were there. Ben had told me what room he and Lanee were staying in. I'd never gone into the fine inn, but Pater must have, for he led me right to the door number I'd told him.

Pater knocked, and in a moment Ben opened the door.

"Hello, Willem. I'm so glad you've come!"

"Ben…this is my pater. Pater, this is Ben."

Ben said, "I am blessed to meet you, sir. This is my wife, Lanee."

As I told Pater what Ben said, Lanee stood up from the couch by the windows, and Pater nodded to her.

"May we offer you both some good grape juice?" she said.

I told Pater what she said.

He said, "Yes, Lanee, that would be very refreshing. The walk here has made me thirsty."

She looked at me and I nodded.

After she served us the cups of juice, we all sat down.

Pater smiled at them and said, "Your message today was quite surprising to me, and the reaction of the people in the Forum even more."

I told Ben what he said. Ben answered, "Jesus came to open our eyes, sir."

Pater studied Ben's face after he knew what he'd said.

"Perhaps you could find another interpreter if you intend to preach in the Forum again. I am a centurion of the Praetorian Guard and I know that what you are doing will not be allowed much longer. My son is too young to decide for himself whether to risk the danger. I would prefer he would not help you tomorrow if you plan to preach there again."

I translated Pater's words. Thinking Ben would be disappointed, I waited, hoping he might try to persuade Pater to let me continue.

Then Ben surprised me. He said, "That is perfectly fine. Before you knocked on our door, Lanee and I were praying. She and I both feel like today was our last day to preach in the Forum. We are asking Jesus to show us what He wants us to do next. If I let you know what it is, and you approve, will you allow Willem to help us again?"

I told Pater, who let out a relieved sigh and smiled at Ben. "He wants to continue, and if I consider it safe, I will allow him."

When I told them what Pater said, Lanee replied, "Good, we will see you tomorrow at your mater's shop, Willem."

After we left, I walked down the dark street home beside Pater feeling like I'd been given a great gift. *Jesus, do you always help this well?* I glanced up at my pater walking along with a calm smile on his lips. I knew he was proud of me, but he couldn't have felt as proud as I. *Jesus, do you see who I am walking beside? It is my pater. Did you hear him with Ben? Wasn't he the best?*

Again, I thought about my talking to Jesus. A voice whispered, *How do you know there's anybody listening to you? You can't believe what everyone tells you. You're being just as foolish to believe in Jesus as the people are who pray to Jupiter and Apollo.*

Pater interrupted the thoughts when he said, "My fellow soldier who came with me today bowed down along with everyone else. He told me later that he was in Palestine when Jesus was crucified. He said the priests bribed the guards not to tell anyone what happened when they guarded Jesus' tomb. He told me Jesus *is* alive, though He has gone back to Heaven."

What he'd said as well as *when* he'd said it made my eyes burn with tears. I took hold of Pater's arm, "My pater, do you believe in Jesus, too?"

Pater stopped and turned to me. "Son, if I did, it would be hard for me to continue doing my job. Rome's gods are those approved of by the Senate and the emperor. I belong to Rome's army. I am not free to believe in or do anything contrary to the laws set by them. But now, I see by your tears that you believe in Him."

I suddenly felt shy. I knew I believed, but I knew I wasn't strong—not like Ben or the others.

We walked on home. Mater had supper waiting for us. She listened as Pater told her of the change in Ben's plans. I could see she was relieved.

What she said next caused both our mouths to fall open— "This Jesus may turn our whole world upside down before He is finished with us."

CHAPTER SEVENTEEN

LANEE, PREACH TO THE CHILDREN!

L ANEE was dreaming of home early the next morning when she heard Jesus say, "Go into all the world, Lanee, and preach to the little ones of my love, and I will be with you." When she opened her eyes she was surprised to see the luxurious surroundings of her room in the Roman inn. The dream had been so real.

She woke up her husband. "Listen, Ben, He said it again!"

"What…who…what did you say, Yona?" Ben answered, not really wanting to open his eyes yet.

She told him the amazing words she'd heard in her sleep. "Eema and I were waiting for Abba out where Jesus was preaching that day. I wanted to speak to Him so I went the same time the eemas were bringing the little children to Him. That's when He said it the first time, Ben. And just now He said it again." She jumped up and began to get dressed. "I believe He's ready for me to start preaching to the children right here in Rome!"

Ben was fully awake now. He laughed and said, "Thank you, Jesus, for directing our steps away from the Forum and to the children!"

Lanee stopped tying her sandal. "Oh my! I know Willem and Elise will help me." She grabbed the other sandal, and said, "Get ready, Ben. Let's go wake up David and Deborah!

Let's get them to pray with us this morning!"

Soon they knocked on their friends' door. David answered with his dark curls falling over his face. Lanee and Ben both laughed. Deborah came and stood behind him, and Lanee excitedly told them the news. "I know that's what He wants me to do. Will you help me? Can we pray together? Will you come over to our room as soon as you get dressed?"

When the four of them knelt and began to pray, the Holy Ghost fell on them, and they all began to speak in the heavenly language He poured into their hearts and mouths. When they arose from prayer, they all felt the awe of being moved on in such a strong way.

"Truly, we are being directed by Jesus into this!" David said.

"And do you remember the new song we wrote last night, David?" asked Deborah with surprise on her face.

"Yes—now it makes sense! Lanee, Ben, it starts out, *Oh, little children, Come unto me! Yea, little children, learn of me.*

"I hope it's all practiced up, for I think you'll be singing it today somewhere in Rome," Ben exclaimed. He put his arm around Lanee and said, "Just what do you think the Lord wants you to preach?"

"It seems right now He wants me to tell them about being with Him, and how it made me feel," she said, remembering it all again. "I'll do it! Come on! Let's go find Willem and Elise!"

~~~

I awoke with all four of them staring down at me. Their faces were alight!

"Willem, we need you!" Ben said.

"Not at the Forum," David added.

"We need you to gather up your friends," Deborah put in.

"Oh, Willem, I've heard from Jesus! Will you help us?"

That was Lanee. Her eyes were glowing down on me. "Sure...yes...I'll be up in a few minutes."

That's when they all turned and went clattering down the stairs.

I jumped up and pulled a clean tunic over my head. *Jesus? Is that how you make people feel when they know you?* As I laced up my sandals, I held my breath hoping to hear His voice in my mind. *Oh, could I hear your voice, someday, Jesus?*

I didn't stop to listen then, for I wanted to know what had excited my four new friends this time. *Didn't Lanee say she'd heard from Jesus?*

Mater had them all eating breakfast. She'd toasted some cheese and bread, and had served them cups of cool grape juice. "Thank you, Mater, for this." I said softly as I slipped in beside her at the counter.

She gave me a cup of juice, and nodded. "Where are you young people going today?" she asked.

"The Lord showed us our work is done for now at the Forum. This morning he has directed us to others. Tell them, Lanee," David said.

Lanee flashed an excited smile and said, "He wants me to preach to the children of Rome!"

Mater and I both cried out, "What?" at the same time.

"Yes. Remember He showed you to me, Willem, in my country, and this morning He reminded me that He wanted me to tell *the little ones* about Him."

After that their questions started flying like bees around

my head. "Willem, where can we gather the children?" "Where can they come and hear Lanee?" "Will you help us gather them?" "Can you interpret for us again?" "Do you think Elise will help us?"

I kept chewing on my bread. When I turned my eyes on Mater she gave me that look she'd given me on the ship when these four were crazily dancing around us.

I swallowed my bread and cried, "Wait!"

They all stopped talking and listened.

"All right. When do you want to start?"

Lanee reached out and touched my hand, "Willem, we only have three more weeks here, and there is so much to do. Can we start today?"

"I'll help you all I can, and I'm sure Elise will too. But we're going to need more help than that. Finish your food now, and let's go."

We left Mater and the shop and walked toward Leo's place. He ran out and joined us, then I whistled for Turk and Blue, and finally we all ended up at Senny's steps.

We sat down on his stoop, and I introduced my friends to each other—Hebrew to Latin, Latin to Hebrew. I explained to my fraters what Lanee wanted to do.

Senny asked, "How about the courtyard between Elise's insula and Rabbi Saul's? No one ever goes there."

"Won't work—the rabbi doesn't want to hear about Jesus."

"What if we went to the cemetery? It's almost always deserted," Leo suggested.

"Maters won't let their children go there," I said.

Blue and Turk put their heads together, then said, "We know where there's a vacant warehouse. It's the one two streets over, Willem. Remember when the last fire burned up that row of apartments? The warehouse wasn't burned, but they moved everything out of it during the fire and no one has moved anything back in."

"Let's go see it!"

I explained it to my Hebrew friends, and we set out for the building. Sure enough it was empty and standing open. We went through the open door into the large high-ceilinged room that echoed our voices as we talked.

"What do you think, Willem?" Ben said as we peered into the dark corners in the back. "Who owns it?"

"I don't know. And I have no idea how to find out. You see the other buildings are still not rebuilt around it." I noticed some spilled beans and a layer of dirty straw covering the cement floor in one corner. The walls were built of strong rough boards. Way up high, spiders had strung their webs over the rafters. Cobwebs, dirt, and all, I liked the feeling of the big room.

We walked back up to the others. They were standing where the sunlight streamed through the open doorway. Ben brushed his hair back and smiled at his wife, "Lanee, let's pray about getting this place for our meetings." The four of them knelt down on the dirty concrete floor and started talking to Jesus.

My fraters were surprised even after I explained what they were doing. "Do they expect a dead man to answer them, Willem?" Turk asked.

We listened, though I was the only one who knew what they were saying. When they stopped, Ben turned to me. "Willem, will you ask the rabbi about this building?"

"Why, Ben? Do you think he knows who owns it?"

"Yes. I felt the Lord say you should ask him."

"I'll go to the store now. Wait here. I'll be right back."

After I told Senny and the others where I was going, I walked toward the rabbi's store. I found him behind the counter waiting on customers.

"Hello, Rabbi. I haven't seen you for awhile."

"Yes, I know, Willem. I heard you're helping Benjamin ben Jacob preach his lies to the Gentiles. Have they got you believing in Jesus Christ now?"

"I like Him, Rabbi. I love to hear about Him. I've never heard about anyone like Him before."

"Well, that's because you don't know any better. What could I do for you today?"

"I came to ask you a question. Do you know who owns the abandoned warehouse two streets over where the insulas were burnt last month?"

"Yes, I do. Why do you want to know?"

"My friends would like to use the building for some gatherings."

"To preach about Jesus?"

"Yes, sir."

"I own the building now."

Uh-oh. Well, I might as well ask. "So…would you let us use it for only a few weeks, Rabbi?"

He didn't smile. It just wasn't like him to be so solemn with me. He studied my eyes and I studied his. Finally he answered me. "I will *rent* it to you…on one condition."

"What is that, Rabbi?"

"That only you will pay the rent."

"Do you mean with the money I have saved?"

"Yes, I do, Chezek. And I would like forty denarii per day."

"Per day?" I knew the money would be gone in less than a week.

"Yes. Take it, or leave it."

"I must talk it over with the friends who have helped me earn the money."

"I will await your decision."

I was totally shocked by my old friend's tone and the price he had given me. I hurried back to the warehouse and quickly told my fraters what the rabbi had said.

Senny said, "You mean that Jesus really told Ben that Rabbi Saul owned this building? That means He can't be dead!"

"Yes, Senny, and the rabbi doesn't believe in Him."

I knew Lanee and the others could tell I was troubled, but I needed to talk it over with Senny and the rest before I could really tell them yes or no about the warehouse.

"But, Willem, what about our plan to move out of Rome? In only a few days our money will all be gone," Blue said, looking unhappy.

"That's why I am asking the four of you first. Do you know of any other place Lanee could meet with the children that's close enough?"

"What about one of our apartments, Willem? A few children could fit there." Turk said.

"I don't believe that is what Lanee has in mind."

I turned to Lanee and the others. I told them that Jesus had surely sent me to Rabbi Saul for he owned the place. They raised their hands and thanked Jesus for showing them.

Then I told them what the rabbi had offered. I could see

they knew why his price was so steep.

Deborah said, "We will give you a raise, starting today, Willem. Instead of ten denarii per day, we will pay you forty."

"It won't work. Rabbi is holding my money. He knows that I couldn't make that much in a day unless you gave it to me."

David asked, "Would you and your friends like to loan your money to us for a few days by paying for the building? We will gladly pay you back before we leave."

"Of course we can do that. But our money will only last a few days. Then what?"

"We will pray that God will change Rabbi's mind and heart by then."

So that's what we did. I went back to the store and told Rabbi to draw out forty denarii of our money to pay for rent on the building for tomorrow. Then we began scouring the insulas around the warehouse for children.

"Tomorrow, there will be a great meeting at the warehouse. Come and hear about the greatest man that ever lived! There will be music. There will be many other children there. Come at the 7th hour to the 9th hour!"

I went to see Rufus. He and some others I knew were throwing a ball around in the courtyard of their insula. "Hey! Ruf! May I join you?"

They opened the circle up for me, and we played awhile. When we took a break, I sat down beside Rufus and said quietly, "I have some news for you, Ruf. Remember what we talked about at Rabbi Saul's store?"

He looked around to make sure none of the other boys were listening. "Yes, I remember."

"The news is there's going to be a meeting tomorrow at the abandoned warehouse. A girl there will tell us about the God that is real. Would you like to come?"

"Will you be there?"

"Yes, in fact Senny, Turk, Blue, and Leo are coming too. How about all your friends here? Ask them to come. It starts at the 7th hour and lasts until the 9th hour."

"I'll ask Mater. I'll tell her you asked me. But I better not tell her what it's about or she might not let me go."

"I'll look for you and your fraters there, Ruf."

"I'll try."

We went everywhere that day. Believing we might only have a few days in the warehouse, I pushed all of us to invite every child we could find.

We met Elise and a group of her girlfriends as they were heading to the insulas toward the Tiber. We raced them and then tried to find more children there than they did. After that we raced to the next apartment house.

That night I lay on my cot with aching leg muscles. I knew we had done our best. What would happen tomorrow?

CHAPTER EIGHTEEN

WILLEM MEETS JESUS

THE warehouse rang with a hundred shrill voices. Lanee and Elise had their heads together up front. Ben motioned us to have the children sit down in rows on the concrete floor. It was all swept clean now, and several oil lamps lit up the dark corners in the back.

Deborah and David came through the sunlit doorway bringing a basket piled high with figs. When they gave them out to the first row, the room quieted down.

I sat down at the end of the first row. Senny went to the back row. I saw him squeezing himself in between two rowdy older boys. Leo, Turk, and Blue had split up to keep an eye on some little boys they knew couldn't sit still for long.

I looked toward the door and saw Rufus and his friends heading in. He gave me a big smile, and they went toward the back.

Lanee and Elise came up to stand in front of the first row. When Lanee began to speak in Hebrew, the children got even quieter. Lanee paused and Elise translated. "Oh, I see you all like sweet figs!" she said. "I'm so glad. But I've come to bring you something even sweeter than that ripe fruit you're eating today."

Lanee spoke again, "My name is Lanee, and I've come all the way from Palestine to bring you news of something sweet. My husband Ben is over by the door, and the bearers of the figs are Deborah and David. Most of you know Elise, my interpreter."

When Elise translated the last part we all laughed. It was funny to hear her speak of herself that way.

Lanee said, "Have you all finished eating? If so, I want to draw your attention to David and Deborah. They want to teach you to sing a pretty song."

Oh, good! I love to hear them sing.

They brought two low stools up in front. David began strumming his harp, and then Deborah let her strong sweet voice ring out in our tongue,

> "Jesus, child of God,
> So fair and pure,
> Let me be a child of yours;
> Jesus, come to me today.
> So I can throw my sin away."

Now came my part. David had asked me to stand and tell the children, "Let's all help Deborah sing it. Ready?"

David strummed the harp a few times then we felt along for the words, trying to sing it with her. She started it over and we did better. The third time was even better. She gave us all a beautiful smile, and I saw the little girls send her one back.

Then David plucked a few brisk chords, and both of them sang joyfully,

"Oh, little children,
Come unto me,
Yea, little children,
Learn of me,
For I am your Saviour
I am your Lord,
And I will always love you,
I give you my Word."

We all joined in and sang it with them many times. Then Deborah helped us sing her part again. Soon we could all sing the whole song easily.

Lanee and Elise returned to the front as Deborah and David carried their stools to the side. Lanee said, "My friends David and Deborah have taught you their song which had a word in it maybe you've never heard or used before. The word is *Jesus*. He is called *Lord.*" Elise spoke it in Latin.

"Maybe you have heard the word *lord* when someone speaks of the emperor or a senator," Lanee continued. "But have any of you ever heard of *the* Lord, whose name is Jesus, before?"

The children shook their heads when Elise interpreted. Lanee continued, "Jesus is in Heaven now," and she pointed up. "But not long ago He lived in Palestine and came to visit us outside my village. I met Him there." Elise translated it. Then Lanee said, "So, who is Jesus? Would you like to know, children?"

When Elise asked them the question, they all cried out, "Yes!"

All of a sudden Lanee's face became bright and merry. She

began to dance around Elise like she did on the boat when she first met me. The children began laughing and cheering.

"Why, He's the Son of the true and the living God!" she cried out. Elise grabbed it right out of the air and with perfect rhythm said it in Latin. Then all us children caught it and threw it back with the same bouncing beat.

Still dancing around Elise, Lanee answered us, her eyes sparkling with joy, "And He has come to save our souls!" Elise gave it to us with a laugh then we echoed her and laughed out too!

Lanee slowed down and stopped before us. "He's sending His Spirit to you little ones in Rome." Elise said it. "He is your Saviour and Lord!" Elise said it. "Will you believe in Him?"

When Elise asked us, we all yelled out loud and strong, "YES!"

Lanee waited until the loud shout died out. Then she said, "I met Him on a hill behind my house. He taught us of His Father, who is God. He healed the sick, raised the dead, and made the blind to see." Elise translated. "He told me to come tell you about Him, and He said He would save you if I did." After Elise said it, she continued, "If you want Him to save you, you may ask Him. He can hear you in Heaven right this moment."

Elise had a startled expression as she translated. Then she fell to her knees, and began to ask Jesus to save her. We all saw her and knew that was what we wanted to do. I knelt and thought of someone wonderful named Jesus above me far away in Heaven. I said, "I want you to save me, Jesus…right now!"

The words *I have done it, Willem,* bloomed up into my mind.

Oh, is it really you, Jesus? Did you hear me, and answer me?

Again words came, *I sent Lanee to you, didn't I?*

My heart turned over with joy. I wanted to run, or shout out what had happened, or do both! I stood up and looked for Lanee. She must have been waiting for me to look at her—for when she saw my face, she began running and dancing again, and suddenly, I did too.

My eyes swept the room and oh, what I saw! Every one of the children were up on their feet, and their skinny little arms were waving in the air. What noises they were making! I opened my mouth and out came a new language I did not know! We were all speaking strange words! What has happened?

The powerful sound continued—I surely didn't want it to end—we just kept crying out the strange sounds. It felt better with every word! My mind went back to Jesus. He must have done this for us. What does it mean?

Finally I was able to stop saying the wonderful new words. Others were quieting, and Ben went to the front and began speaking. I ran up beside him to interpret. He said, "This is the Comforter that Jesus sent to us after He went back to Heaven. His name is the Holy Ghost."

I watched many of the children repeat the name quietly after I translated.

Elise waved her hand at Ben. She asked in Hebrew, "Why did we speak words we do not know?"

I interpreted her question for the children. They all nodded their heads—it was their question.

Ben answered, "God, Jesus' Father, wants you to understand that it is the great Holy Ghost that is speaking *through* you, and not just *you* speaking." I told them what he said. His voice rose with excitement when he added, "He wants you to know the Holy Ghost has come to you, and now lives inside of you!"

I interpreted it with my own excitement. Suddenly the children stood up again, and began worshiping. *I've found the real God! OH, He is so real in this room!* The Holy Ghost began pouring His words out of my mouth again! *Oh, my wonderful invisible God!*

CHAPTER NINETEEN

MARCUS ANICIA

THE few days that Lanee preached in the warehouse were the most exciting days I'd ever lived in Rome. More and more children came to the warehouse to hear about Jesus and to experience the Holy Ghost. Again Leo, Senny, Turk, Blue, and I combed the city for more girls and boys. Elise and her girls were out doing the same thing.

Besides the children, maters and paters were standing around the back walls listening to Lanee's stories about Jesus and the pretty music David and Deborah taught us.

"Mater, will you come to the warehouse tomorrow?" I said as I swept out the cheese shop before we closed. "I think you will want to hear what Lanee is telling us about Jesus."

"I could hear you children singing way over here yesterday. I loved it! I think I'll just close up early tomorrow and come."

"Do you think Pater could come?"

"Why don't you ask him tonight? He's coming to eat with us."

That night Pater showed up with another legionnaire. It wasn't the same soldier who came with him to the Forum. This one was burly, and when he removed his helmet, a curly mop of grey-streaked black hair appeared. He reminded me of someone. But, who was it?

"Serena and Willem, I would like you to meet my new optio for our century, Marcus Anicia. He wanted to taste your

159

good cooking, Serena, so I invited him. I know you always have plenty prepared."

Mater gave him a pretty smile and said, "We're so glad you came, Marcus, and especially tonight. We are having Lucius' favorite roast and gravy."

Marcus said in a soft gravelly voice, "I have really looked forward to this meal all day long." He looked me over, and I thought he might hug me for a moment. "Willem, I see you have your pater's strong shoulders. Do you also want to be a centurion some day?"

Pater said, "Perhaps Willem will not become a soldier like me. He would be a valuable one though, for he has a real knack for learning languages."

I was glad Pater answered for me, for since I met Jesus, I didn't know at all what I might do. I wasn't even sure I could leave Rome now. I was thinking of that as we gathered around the table upstairs for our meal.

Marcus and Pater really dug into the juicy roast. It seemed that Marcus might be enjoying it even more than Pater. I decided to ask both of them to our meeting tomorrow.

"Pater, has Mater told you about our meeting with the children at the warehouse?"

"Yes, she did last night. She said the whole building was probably filled up with children for the last two days."

"I have been translating there. I didn't think you would mind since they weren't preaching in the Forum."

He didn't say anything but just kept on chewing, so I said, "I want you to come and hear Lanee, Pater. She is telling us about Jesus. It's so wonderful…" Then I turned to Marcus and said, "I wish you would come too, sir."

Pater answered, "Since I am charged to keep the peace in Rome, and I have heard from your mater it is getting quite noisy over there, it just may be my duty to come and inspect what is going on. Then I'll know for sure if it's wise for you to continue to translate, son. Would you like to come with me tomorrow, Optio Anicia?"

"I *would* like to find out what the children are doing. Are Lanee and her husband from Palestine? My post was once in Palestine…" Marcus chewed his roast with a faraway look in his eyes. When he noticed we were staring at him, he turned red and smiled at us all.

Pater said, "I have heard that many people have gathered near Julius Caesar every day hoping Ben will return to preach again. I guess word hasn't got out that there's preaching in the warehouse. Have any other people shown up besides children, Willem?"

"Yes, sir. The parents and other grown-ups have been standing around the walls near the back. But Lanee mostly wants to preach to the children. She said Jesus told her to."

Marcus said, "It does sound interesting."

Pater replied, "We will see for ourselves tomorrow, Optio Anicia." Then Pater changed the subject by asking Mater how many customers she'd had in the shop and did she need to restock her cheeses. I looked over at Marcus. He chewed slowly and stared at the wall opposite him. He was not thinking of Mater's cheese stock. *Who does he remind me of?*

Later I lay on my cot remembering the thrill of Jesus talking to me in my heart. I thought of the way the strange words formed in my mouth and how it felt to speak them. As if God were praying for me. As if God were saying the wonderful things I'd like to say to Him.

Jesus, will you talk to me again? I really want to get to know you. It doesn't matter if I can't see you. All our Roman gods are there for us to see, but they have never reached out to me. You have, and I want to hear your voice again.

I lay there listening. Suddenly I felt the words come again to my mind. I didn't want to wake Mater, so I whispered them. Lanee said it was the Holy Ghost praying. She said the Holy Ghost was also God, as Jesus and His Father are God. I didn't quite know what she meant, but as the words rolled out of my mouth, it seemed totally all right. God isn't like Jupiter and Julius Caesar—so dead. He is a living God—way above and beyond my understanding. *Yet, He loves me. I feel it so real—He loves me.*

After the words stopped, I guess I fell asleep, for the next thing I knew Mater was calling my name.

"Come help me awhile before the meeting. We need to sell enough cheese this morning for the whole day."

I worked and talked to Jesus in my mind. *Will Pater and Mater believe in you? Will Marcus?* Again I tried to place why he looked so familiar. I liked him, and it seemed he and Pater were good friends. Were they friends in Gaul?

Jesus, will you help us in the meeting this afternoon? Will you be with us again? I love you, Lord Jesus!

Mater and I finished up, and she went upstairs to arrange her hair and change clothes. I hurried over to find Senny and my fraters. We headed to an insula where we'd never looked for children. Soon we had a dozen new children following us to the warehouse. Two of their maters trailed behind us.

As we neared the building the noise of hundreds of

children's voices met us. The whole place was buzzing. We came in just as Lanee and Elise asked everyone to sit down. Some of the maters brought baskets of sweets to pass down the lines of children. As they picked out their little cakes and began to eat, the room quieted.

Blue came up to me and motioned for me to step outside with him. I followed wondering what he wanted.

He took me around the corner of the building. Then he said, "I'm not staying for the meeting."

"Yeah, do you have something else you need to do?"

"No, I just don't want to be here."

"What are you saying, Blue?"

"It's no use, Willem. I can't feel what all of you are feeling. I've gone along with it until now, because Turk *did* feel something—he's really happy—but I can't sit through it today." Blue's eyes were flat and sad. "Tell Turk I went home, if he asks you."

I watched him leave.

Jesus, what should I do?

I could hear the contented murmuring of the children inside enjoying their cakes. Again my heart leapt at the thought of Jesus being in our meeting. So I went back in, whispering, "Jesus, help my frat."

I remembered that Pater and Marcus were coming. I noticed Mater standing with Elise's mater in the back. I went to Ben and said, "My pater and another legionnaire are coming today. I invited them." Ben nodded and went to tell the others.

I returned to my place in the front row in time to see Pater and Marcus step into the door and remove their helmets. Pater smiled at me then I saw him searching the back for

Mater. Marcus ran his fingers through his thick hair and looked all around. I saw him scan all the children then he saw Lanee and Ben. David and Deborah were sitting on their stools behind them. David got up to get his harp, and suddenly I knew who Marcus resembled—it was David! As swiftly as that thought filled my mind, I looked back and saw Marcus thinking the same thing. His face was turning a deep red!

David retrieved his harp and sat down with Deborah, taking her hand in his. They laughed about something to each other then they both looked out at the teeming mob of children. David's gaze swept the crowd then he looked toward the door where Pater and Marcus were still standing. I saw David's mouth fall open.

Then Deborah saw David's expression. She followed his gaze, and her mouth fell open too. About that time Pater turned toward Mater and touched Marcus' arm to follow him. Obedient to his superior, Marcus tore his eyes from David's and moved with him.

I was so curious about what this all meant, I almost forgot why we had come. Marcus and David had to be related! Were they father and son, and were they seeing each other for the first time as Pater and I did? I felt tears begin in my eyes.

Lanee and Elise moved in front of us.

Lanee called out, "It's wonderful that you all have come today! We welcome you children, and your maters and paters!" Elise translated, raising her squeaky voice just like Lanee.

"And now, let's ask Jesus to be with us today. Would you like Him to bless you children?"

When we heard Elise's translation, all of us cried, "YES!"

Lanee prayed, and after Elise said it in Latin, she asked David and Deborah to bring their song.

David carried his stool and the harp. His shocked expression had given way to a happy faraway look. He motioned for me to come to interpret for him. Then he said, "My eema and I used to sing this song together in Palestine. How I wish she were here with me now. Children, today Jesus has given me a great gift. My wife Deborah and I will sing about how great a Saviour He is." I interpreted, looking out above the children's heads. Marcus' eyes were glued to the young version of himself.

David strummed his harp, and called out in Latin,
"Jesus is great and wonderful,"
Deborah replied in her lovely way,
"Yet, He even loves me!"
David cried in an even more thrilling voice,
"Jesus is the Son of God,"
Smiling, Deborah replied,
"Still He cares about me!"
David rapped on the strings and cried,
"Jesus died and rose again,"
Deborah answered,
"He did it just for me!"
Then their voices blended in beautiful harmony,
"It's just that He's so strong and good,"
"He saved and set me free!"

As the last note died out, David spoke in Hebrew, "Come now, and sing with us! Boys sing behind me, and girls sing behind my wife!" I echoed him in Latin. David sang the first line, and the boys followed him. Deborah sang hers and then the girls sang it. After a few times of singing the song like that, the boys began to sing with David, and the girls sang with Deborah.

I could hear a bass voice booming from the back—it was Marcus! David held his head up singing with all his power, his eyes shining toward the soldier back there. When I looked behind me again, Marcus' face had broken into a beautiful smile. Then I turned and saw David singing with tears on his cheeks and a white-toothed grin lighting up his handsome face.

"Jesus is great and wonderful,"

"Yet He even loves me!"

David put his harp down as the children sang on,

"Jesus is the Son of God,"

"Still He cares about me!"

He grabbed Deborah's hand and headed around the rows of children. When Marcus saw him coming, he looked at Pater then began making his way toward his son. They held each other's eyes.

We children sang,

"Jesus died and rose again,"

"He did it all for me!"

When David was almost there he dropped Deborah's hand and opened his arms. All of us boys sang out,

"It's just that He's so strong and good," and right when the girls answered us,

"He saved and set me free!"

Marcus stretched out his powerful arms and engulfed David, who buried his tearful face in his neck.

Our eyes had followed David all the way back, and when we saw the big graying soldier hugging our David, we began cheering the roof off! Many of the children were probably soldiers' children too. We didn't know all about David and his pater, but, I, for one, knew how good it felt to finally be in my own pater's arms.

Suddenly Lanee called out, "God is your Heavenly Father and has been looking for you all your life. If you want Him to come to you, believe in His Son, Jesus Christ."

Elise called out the translation.

"Jesus said, 'I go to my Father and your Father, to my God and your God.' Jesus went back to Heaven where the Father is. He will help you meet Him today!"

After Elise translated it, Lanee took her hand and knelt down. It just seemed right to go down on our knees too. She prayed. "Father, we need you. We are weak and unable to make any sense out of the world we're living in. Please come to us and help us. We ask you earnestly, Father, in Jesus' name."

When Elise spoke the Latin words, the same Holy Ghost

we felt that first day came again! We spoke in tongues as He moved on us. It was like the waves of the Great Sea moving over us. We felt our Father's presence, then we heard Him moving over the back of the room, and then the wave broke over us again…and again! How many times this happened I do not know.

And then the storm quieted. We got up and began talking in low tones to each other. I went to the back and found Mater and Pater kneeling beside each other. Their arms were entwined and they were smiling. I knelt in front of them seeking their eyes. Pater and I smiled at each other, then Mater.

"Pater, did you…?"

"Yes, son, I did!"

And Mater said, "And so did I, my son Willem!"

CHAPTER TWENTY

THE RABBI'S CHALLENGE

WHEN Pater and Marcus left for the camp, David and Deborah came home with Mater and me. I wanted to ask him question after question. I felt different about him, just knowing that his pater was a Roman. It made him feel like a real brother to me.

"Did you know your pater was in Rome when you came, David?" I asked.

David still looking amazed answered, "I hoped to find him. My eema had told me his name, but didn't know any more about him. She was certain he was still alive."

Mater said in halting Hebrew, "Marcus seems like a fine man, David."

David looked at her gratefully. "I thought that too."

Deborah said, "How much you look like your abba, David."

"Yes, and I always thought I looked like Eema's family. Abba is coming to see me later tonight. He told me that in Hebrew! There are so many things I want to know. And how I wish Eema were here. How I wish I could tell her now what has happened. My eema has always loved my abba."

Soon they left for their room. Pater planned to return later, so Mater and I rested awhile. She seemed to want to be alone with her thoughts.

I marveled at the great things that had happened today. *Both Mater and Pater believe in Jesus. Both of them have the Holy Ghost. Oh, Jesus! How wonderful you are to me, my*

169

Savior! What else can I do for you? What would you like for me to do, Lord?

"Feed my sheep." The Hebrew words came so soon after my question, I almost missed them. But I knew who had spoken them. It was Jesus.

And I answered back quickly, Y*es, Lord, I will, if you will help me.*

"I will never leave thee nor forsake thee," He said again in the language of the Jews.

I breathed out a sigh of relief—for I had wondered if one day I would have to say goodbye to Jesus—maybe when Lanee and the others left. Now that I knew He was with me for good, I felt a big load lift off of me. *Do you mean I'll always be able to talk to you and have you with me, Lord? Perfectus!*

I guess I took a nap after that and Mater did too. Pater came back and woke us both. He had a big smile on his face as he bent over my cot. "Son, get up, let's talk about this Jesus. Let's talk about this Holy Ghost. I want to know everything you know."

And I did just that, finishing by saying, "And so, Pater, Jesus is the Son of the God of the Hebrews. His name is Jehovah. He made all of us, and everything we see all around us."

"That means all our gods are false gods, Willem."

"Yes, sir. Before we found each other, I was so hungry for help that I tried to reach them one day. They are only concrete and marble statues, Pater. I found that out."

"What did you want them to help you with, son?"

"I thought you didn't want to be my pater. I thought we couldn't be together because you are a soldier."

"Well, it *is* true that I'm not allowed to marry. And I'm sorry that Mater and I have had to live in such a manner up until now. But I'm not sorry that I have you. And I will be your pater in every way for as long as I live, Willem. I only have a little while left in the army, then Mater and I will marry and we will all live together. I'm sorry I left you without me for so long. I will try to make it up to you."

"How great it is to have you now!" I went and hugged him to me.

He hugged me back then said, "We must learn how our Lord Jesus would have us to serve Him. Do you know how, son?"

I thought of what Jesus had spoken to me. But I didn't think it was meant for me to tell Pater then. So I said, "I am only learning as a boy. Perhaps you could ask Ben or David. I only know a little."

He nodded that he understood.

Then I remembered, "Oh, yes, they told me they have scrolls with Jesus' words written on them. Maybe they would let us see them. I learned how to read their writing at Rabbi Saul's shop."

"Willem, we must find out all we can before they leave."

"I'll ask Ben if I can see them tomorrow."

"Pater, tomorrow will be our last day in the warehouse."

"Why is that?"

"Our money will have run out."

"Oh?"

"We, that is, Senny, Leo, Turk, Blue, and I are renting the building. I believe we only have enough money for one more day. It costs forty denarii per day."

"Per day? Who is renting it to you at such a high price?"

"Rabbi Saul. And, he won't let anyone pay for it but us."

I began at the beginning and told Pater about our saving up to find us a place outside of Rome, and how we had given the money to the rabbi to hold for us. I told him how Ben preached about Jesus, and Rabbi Saul didn't like it. "So, I believe he has charged us the high rent to limit the meetings to only these few."

"We must find another place. Tomorrow, I will help you."

"Do you have any ideas? Deborah has enough money to rent a place, if we knew of one."

"Not yet, but I'll ask around."

After Pater left, I asked Mater if I could go to Rabbi Saul's store. Mater had heard what I told Pater and she said, "Why are you going?"

"I want to make sure we have enough for the rent tomorrow. Deborah paid me for the last three days, so I have a little more if we are short."

"All right, son. Let Jesus show you how to handle it."

I stared at Mater after she said that. How quickly she had found the secret and begun to live in it. I gave her a big smile and left for the store.

Dark had descended on Rome. I knew not to dawdle, but to get down the street as quickly as my feet would carry me. When I got there the store was lit up with many lamps. Even though he would be closing soon, Rabbi knew that many shoppers could come at the very last as they did many nights.

Rabbi looked up at me with a sad expression when I walked in. "Hello, Willem. I was wondering if I would see you today."

"I have brought my pay for three days so we can have at

least one more day in the warehouse."

"I have been hearing the children singing every day. I have heard another sound which I can't say I have understood."

"You would be welcome to come tomorrow, if you would like to, Rabbi."

"I counted your money today, and I needed ten more denarii for tomorrow. So, if you'll give me that, you may have the meeting tomorrow. Then you must move."

I handed him the money. He studied my eyes as I gave it to him.

Tell him, I heard Jesus whisper.

"The sound you are hearing are all the children and parents speaking in a language they do not know. It is because the Holy Ghost has come and filled us."

He reeled as if I had pulled back my fist and hit him.

"We are given great joy when He fills our mouths. We know that God is showing us His mighty power to save us and to help us to know Him."

I called God "Elohim" when I said it.

Rabbi Saul said, "You don't know Him, boy. You are being deceived."

Before I turned to leave, I said, "Come and see, Rabbi."

CHAPTER TWENTY-ONE

EEMA LIRA

SHE heard footsteps coming toward the door. Turning from the window that looked out on the Romanum Forum, Eema Lira stood ready. *Will they be glad to see me? Oh, I shouldn't have come...*

David and Deborah opened the door of their lovely room. "Eema? Oh, Eema!" David ran to her and caught her up in his arms. "The Lord must have heard my thoughts today and brought you here. But how could He so soon, Eema?"

Deborah got her arms around them both, and they all burst into tears. Deborah whispered to her, "Oh, Eema Lira, how did you know?"

"Know what, my daughter?" Eema dropped her arms and stood back from them. "All I know is I haven't been able to sleep since you left. I could think of nothing but David so far away in Rome without me. Deborah, we have never been apart. After a week of that I could not stand it. I asked Yosef to loan me the money to sail here, and here I am!" Then she looked worried. "I hope you don't mind my coming, for I know it is your wedding trip."

David and Deborah both hugged her again, and David said over her head, "Eema, God has directed you."

"Why do you think so, son?"

"Eema, we have a great surprise for you. The Lord has just given it to us today. But first would you like to get cleaned up from your journey? Deborah will help you. I have an errand I must attend to, and while I am out I will tell the servants to bring you a tub and prepare a meal for us to be ready when I return."

Eema studied her son's beloved face, and said, "Yes, son, the journey has been long, and a bath would feel so good. But can't you tell me the surprise now? Is it about Lanee and Ben, or about you two?"

David thought he knew what she meant but chose to not comment. He kissed his pretty eema's cheek and winked at Deborah as he kissed her and left.

It wasn't long before the servants brought in a tub and poured in steaming jars of water. When Eema Lira let herself down in the soothing warm water, her body relaxed for the first time since leaving Arbela. Deborah helped to wash and rinse her hair.

Soon she was wrapped up in a large towel. She looked over at Deborah who was laying out a beautiful soft lavender tunic and stola.

"May I loan you one of my favorite tunics, my mother?" Deborah sweetly asked. "The color will suit you, and will be perfect for your first night in Rome."

"If you wish, Deborah. But I brought my clothes along, and I have some nice things. I even sewed a few on the ship as we sailed."

"I'm sure they are nice, but actually I have wanted you to have this one ever since David and I were married. I knew it was made for your coloring. Also, Eema, here is some lovely smelling perfume. Will you try it on your wrists? David thinks I am sweeter when I wear it."

"Oh, daughter, you are too good to me. I have burst into

your wedding trip because I missed my boy so, and you are spoiling me with dresses and perfume. Now, what? Oh, those elegant sandals? Yes, dear, they do go with the tunic."

Deborah smiled as she held them for her and tied the laces. "Now, will you allow me to arrange your hair? It is just about dry. Would you like to wear it down or up, for your first night in Rome?"

Lira looked into Deborah's smiling eyes, and wondered. *Why is she set on making me so beautiful tonight?* "What do *you* think, child?"

Deborah walked around her studying the clothes on Lira's slim figure then said, "It must be down with curls over your shoulders." She gently combed Eema Lira's hair into a becoming style.

Eema smiled at her reflection in the mirror. "Will David recognize his eema?" she asked, and laughed with Deborah.

Just as they finished, the servants came to remove the bath. More servants came with trays of food.

Eema Lira said, "Can we eat all this?"

"Yes, I am very hungry. We worked hard for Jesus today." Deborah replied.

"You did? Tell me. And oh, I want to help tomorrow. I'll do anything you need me to do. I'm so glad I'm here, my sweet daughter."

Just then heavy footsteps sounded in the hall. A knock came, and David called through the door, "Are you ready, Eema?"

She looked surprised that he called to her instead of Deborah, and said, "Yes, son."

Looking from the middle of the room, she saw David and

then a man coming in behind him. It was another David. *NO! IT IS MARCUS!* Suddenly her legs couldn't hold her up.

When they saw her falling, they both reached out their arms. After all the years apart, they met in one big hug! And Deborah wrapped her fair arms around her new family and hugged them even closer.

It was a night of which Lira had dreamed many times. Only better, for she had never pictured Deborah in her dream. *My Marcus and my David!* For the first time she had the privilege of seeing her husband engaging in conversation with their son. It was so amazing that she was with him again, hearing his voice. She listened to his hesitant Hebrew, but it seemed he recalled their language more and more as they ate. He had spoken it very well when they were married so long ago.

He laughed, and she felt a joy that she hadn't felt for many years. All the years were still unexplained, but somehow the need to know had melted away. It was enough to be with him again.

David and Deborah asked to be gone for awhile so they could tell Ben and Lanee that she had come.

After they left, Marcus raised his eyes and met Lira's. "I am remembering how to speak with you again. And the one thing I really want to say is, will you forgive me, Lira?"

"I-I have missed you so, Marcus."

"Yes, I have been a fool. Will you forgive me for leaving you back there?"

"I never have forgotten you. I have always been true to you," Lira said in a low voice.

Marcus groaned. Then he said, "Will you forgive me, sweet wife?"

"Do you like our son, my husband?"

"I knew him the moment I saw him, even though I didn't know we had a son."

"He is so much like you. He has been such a comfort to me."

Marcus groaned again. "Will you forgive me, Lira?"

Lira touched his hand and said, "You are my husband. I will not blame you for anything ever, for I love you dearly. I knew you were alive somewhere, and I have always believed I would see you again. God has given me this! So, now, my husband, what would you like for us to do from here on?"

He moved his face closer to hers and asked, "What if it pleases me to keep you here with me in Rome? What if I never want to spend another day separated from you for the rest of my life?"

She gave him her sweetest smile and said, "Then, dear husband, I will be pleased to stay with you."

Marcus stood and took her hand. When she stood, he took her into his arms and held her to him.

She felt his strong arms wrapped around her. She looked up into his eyes and thought for a moment. Then she asked, "Have you met Jesus our Saviour, Marcus?"

"I learned of Him for the first time today," he answered with a smile. "And just today I asked Him to be my Lord."

Lira laid her head down on his chest with a great contented sigh. Finally her long dark night was over.

CHAPTER TWENTY-TWO

WILLEM PREACHES

I T was our last meeting at the warehouse, and I had no idea of where we could go after this. Lanee and Ben had another week left in Rome. More children were here today, and more grown-ups lined the back walls.

Jesus, where can we go? How can we go on without Lanee and Ben? Why have you told me to feed your sheep?

I watched David and Deborah arrive with his pater and a pretty woman walking beside him. Pater and Mater were already in the back, and I saw Marcus heading toward them, but the woman stayed with David. Just before Lanee and Elise came to the front, I saw another grown-up coming through the door—Rabbi Saul. Behind him were Simeon and his wife. They looked around and then headed toward the back. Rabbi Saul passed near me. I looked into his eyes for a moment. They seemed sad.

Today big baskets of fruits were passed around. The children were excited with the figs, grapes, and dates they were given. As usual they quieted down as they ate. I looked around and located Senny and Leo. I nodded at Turk as he came through the door. Blue wasn't with him. I tried not to worry over my frat.

Lanee and Elise came forward. "We welcome you in the name of Jesus Christ our Lord! How we praise the Lord for the blessing He gave us yesterday. Do you want to be blessed again today, children?"

When Elise translated it in her high excited voice, they cried out, "Yes!" From the back I heard, "Praise the Lord! Hallelujah! Oh, yes!"

"We have a wonderful addition to our team from Palestine today. David, come and introduce her to the children." The children clapped when Elise said it in Latin.

David and Deborah came with the new woman between them. I went up front to translate. David said, "I was very blessed to be reunited with my abba as all of you witnessed yesterday. Then my eema surprised me by meeting us at the inn where we are staying. Eema, I would like you to meet Jesus' children in Rome!" She smiled as I translated his words. "Eema will sing for you today. She will sing a beautiful song in our Hebrew language." I told the children. Then David said, "These are the words:

> Holy Child of God, without you I'd be lost,
> I'd never know my Father, never
>   sing His praise;
> You have gone before me, washed my sin away,
> Given me an open door,
>   to let His child come in.
> Holy Child of God,
> My Jesus,
> Without you I'd be lost."

I felt the joy of the words as I translated them line by line to the staring children. Then David's eema began to sing as he softly strummed the harp. I stood to the side as she sang. Her voice seemed to come from that far away place called

Palestine. It seemed to come from great sadness turned into wondrous joy. I could have listened to it for hours.

I peered over the children to where Rabbi Saul stood. His eyes seemed to be turned inward. I knew this man, how jolly and good he'd been to me all my life. Didn't he hear the truth of her song?

When she came to the last line, I heard David's true bass voice join her singing, "Holy Child of God, My Jesus, without you I'd be lost."

Suddenly, I began speaking. "You are here for a reason. God has called you to give up your pride in your knowledge of words, and to begin to learn of Him through His Son, the Word made flesh. He has promised you His help, because you are His chosen. Yes, My help is offered today, and you are blessed to receive it by My Spirit."

I had spoken in Hebrew. I was shocked at myself. But I had no time to worry, for there was a commotion in the back. The three Jews were down on their knees. Their hands were raised, and tears were falling from their eyes.

How had this happened? I hurried to the back, and knelt down by my friends. My tears were flowing too. Mater and Pater were with us.

Rabbi Saul pulled out a linen handkerchief from his belt. He blew His nose then cried some more. Simeon and his wife were both still sniffling. I said, "Rabbi, are you all right?"

"Yes, my Chezek. I am finally all right."

The children had all turned around and were quietly listening. Many did not understand what we said, but they knew something amazing had happened.

The rabbi lifted his voice so all could hear him. He

spoke in clear Latin. "Today I had come to challenge your work. I was ready to tell all you children to go back home and forget all that you've heard here. Before I left my store, Elohim spoke a word in my ear. It was, "Chezek." In our language it means strength and help. It is my name for this young man, Willem. When I heard the whisper of my God in my ear, I was thrilled for I have not heard that whisper in many years. I steeled my heart when the lovely daughter of Palestine sang her song. But then Chezek spoke to me! He spoke to my heart the Words of my God! I will follow His Son! Lord Jesus, forgive me!"

When he began to wail toward God, all the children began to praise the Lord, and the Holy Ghost fell again. The words rolled out of my mouth over and over, and soon I heard Rabbi and his family speaking new words given by the Holy Ghost! Pater and Mater, David and Deborah, Ben and Lanee, and Marcus and David's eema were with us and all the children—Senny, Turk, Leo, all of us were shouting the glory of God in the pure words the Holy Ghost gave!

CHAPTER TWENTY-THREE

RABBI SAUL AND BEN

A FTER all the children and their parents had left for home, I asked Mater if I could wait for Lanee and Ben. I had seen Rabbi Saul speak to Ben right before he went out the door.

"Ben, I want to go with you," I said.

"Where, Willem?"

"To talk to the rabbi. I need to hear what he says to you."

"How did you know I was going?"

"I saw him speaking to you. When are you going? Will you take me with you?"

Ben brushed his dark hair back from his eyes and said, "You really like to know about everything that's going on around you, don't you Willem?"

I said, "That's been my way of making it in Rome up to now."

"All right, if you must, come along. He didn't say *not* to bring you."

"When are you going?"

"After his store closes tonight. I'll come by for you."

As I headed toward the shop alone, my mind was buzzing. I couldn't wait to hear Rabbi talk about Jesus. *Does he really love you now, Jesus? What will he say about the Holy Ghost? What about his Torah? Does it go along with believing in you, Jesus? Or will he have to give it up?* I remembered speaking the words out in the service, but I didn't understand what I'd said. *Is Jesus' Father really the same God as Rabbi's Elohim?*

Mater had the shop open when I got there. I helped her wait on customers and restock the shelves. Pater had gone back to the camp and was not coming back later—he had to make up for being gone during the meeting.

"Mater, may I go with Ben to visit Rabbi Saul tonight? He is going after Rabbi closes his store."

"Oh, they are meeting? Well, yes, you may. Really, I'd like to be there myself, but I'd probably not understand what they say. I can understand them sometimes, but sometimes I get quite lost when they're talking fast. Do you think Rabbi Saul will apologize to Ben?"

"I hope so."

"Well, make sure to stay with Ben, and come directly back when you finish there."

There she goes again!

No, there I go again. Mater knows I'm only eleven. But I'm sure I can take care of myself. Yet the fact is I am just a boy in this meanest of cities!

I leaned the broom on the counter and went to Mater to hug her good and hard. *See, my mother, I am big and strong!*

She hugged me back, and looked into my eyes, hers soft with tears.

Then I felt like her little boy again. *Which am I?*

Both, I guess.

The time seemed to crawl before Ben came looking for me. Finally we walked down the dimly lit streets. I was on the alert thinking a robber might jump out from one of the darkened storefronts and attack us. Soon the wagons would rumble down the streets again. We walked on silently toward the store.

Ben said, "Rome sure is quiet tonight."

Rabbi Saul met us at the door, "Come in, you boys! I could hardly wait for you to come. I'm glad you came along, Chezek, I have much to tell you, too."

Simeon and his wife, Rachel, were behind him. Simeon clapped me on the shoulder, and Rachel gave us a glad smile.

Rabbi said, "Let's go upstairs. I want to show you something," as he led us through the thick back curtain of the store.

We went up the stairs I had climbed before, but this time we turned to the right at the top of the stairs. The door Rabbi opened led into another red-carpeted room. Several flickering lamps lit it up. Mounted on the walls were storage spaces filled with many scrolls. Rabbi held out his arm with a grand gesture, saying, "This is my collection of the Holy Scriptures, Benjamin ben Jacob. The Torah has its own room, as you know, Chezek. Tonight I wanted to read some from our other prophets' writings. Please have a seat. Simeon, will you help me?"

We sat down on the stools around a table in the middle of the room.

"First of all, Simeon, will you bring me the Prophet Esaiah's scroll?"

Rabbi Saul expertly unwound the scroll that Simeon unwrapped and placed on the table before him. Simeon helped him on the other end. He laid his brass pointer on the very words he wanted after rolling the scroll almost half way. "Here it is: listen! 'Whom shall he teach knowledge? and whom shall he make to understand doctrine? them that are weaned from the milk, and drawn from the breasts. For precept must be upon precept; line upon line; here a little, and there a little: For with stammering lips and another tongue will he speak to this people. To whom he said, This is the rest wherewith ye may cause the weary to rest; and this is the refreshing: yet they would not hear. But the word of the LORD was unto them precept upon precept, precept upon precept; line upon line, line upon line; here a little, and there a little; that they may go, and fall backward, and be broken, and snared, and taken.' Now Simeon, get Prophet Joel's scroll."

When the much smaller scroll was unrolled, Rabbi read as he pointed out the words, "'And it will come to pass afterward, that I will pour out my spirit upon all flesh; and your sons and your daughters shall prophesy, your old men shall dream dreams, your young men shall see visions: And also upon the servants and upon the handmaids in those days will I pour out my spirit...And it shall come to pass, that whosoever shall call on the name of the LORD shall be delivered:'"

Then Rabbi Saul moved away from the scroll, and surprised us by kneeling with his hands stretched out to Ben. "Benjamin ben Jacob, I beg your pardon for the way I've treated you. I now understand that my old friend Yosef well knew what he was doing when he sent you to me. Will you forgive me?"

Ben came off his seat and knelt with him. "Thank God," he prayed. "Thank God. Yes, in the name of Jesus Christ, I forgive you!"

Simeon, who hadn't said a word, then spoke. "Rachel and I have spent our nights in this room searching the scrolls after you preached about Jesus to us, Benjamin. We have found much evidence to point us to His being our Messiah. Oh, in Zechariah's prophecy, my heart was touched when the prophet said, 'And I will pour upon the house of David, and upon the inhabitants of Jerusalem the spirit of grace and of supplications: and they shall look upon me whom they have pierced, and they shall mourn for him as one mourneth for his only son, and shall be in bitterness for him, as one that is in bitterness for his firstborn.'

"I told my abba what we found, and he agreed that it was possible, especially when we read in Esaiah that He would be 'led as a lamb to the slaughter.' We have always looked for the Messiah to be a mighty conqueror. But the scriptures point to His suffering a brutal death as we had heard that Jesus suffered. In the children's meeting this day we were convinced. Today we were changed, as it says in the Prophet Zechariah's scroll, 'Not by might, nor by power, but by my spirit, saith the Lord of hosts.' He has chosen to help us believe and to become the vessels of His Spirit, and now we *know* that Jesus Christ *is* the Son of the Blessed, and our Messiah!"

That was when I had the chance to ask my question. "Why did you not know about Elohim's Son until now?"

Ben spoke, "If I may, I would like to answer Willem's

question. Our scriptures declare that our God is one God. We have always considered *that* our first and foremost principle. Yet our word for God, *Elohim,* is a plural word. Is God plural? Yes, for the Spirit of truth, which is the Holy Ghost, is teaching us that God is not only our Father, but He is one with our Lord Jesus His Son, and also one with our Comforter, the Holy Ghost. He is and always has been plural. Before Jesus Christ came to reveal God to us, we did not understand it from the scriptures, Willem. But Jesus came to reveal who God is. Without Jesus we can't know our God. Without Jesus we can't be filled with the Holy Ghost. That's why we haven't known before now."

Rabbi Saul said, "I thought I knew so much, Benjamin. All 'precept upon precept, here a little, there a little.' When Elohim spoke to me through you today, Chezek, He drew me to a living relationship with Himself, through believing in His Son. I accepted it, and now I have the whole of my plural God—the Father, the Son, and the Holy Ghost! Thank you, my God, thank you!"

We all began to thank Him along with Rabbi Saul. I looked around and realized that God had given me my desire and let me into the family. I wasn't a son or a grandson like I'd wanted to be, but I was a brother.

Then Rabbi Saul took the lamp and led us back downstairs to the store. He picked up a large basket in the storage room and carried it to the front. He began gathering sweets from all his displays—honeyed wafers, fruited pastries, sugary dates. He said, "Tomorrow the children will be quieted with *my* treats!"

"But, Rabbi—" I remembered how my money had all run out.

"The Lord Jesus has changed my mind, Chezek. I will refund you all yours and your fraters' money, and the children may use the warehouse to meet with Jesus, my Father, and the blessed Holy Ghost from now on. It will be theirs permanently." Then he handed me a jelly-filled tart. "Here, try this. Do you think they'll like it?"

As I chewed the delicious treat, I asked, "Rabbi, will you come tomorrow? Will you come and give the children their treats? It would mean so much more to them if you and Simeon gave them out."

"Yes, Willem, and I will bring others in our synagogue, if they will come when I tell them how Jesus has saved me. Jesus is too great a gift to hide from others."

Ben and I walked home among the men driving the wagons into the town. Ben was all eyes to see this new thing. As for me, I felt like I was in a dream, floating a few inches above the sidewalk. How could all this good be happening here in Rome? Many children and their parents knew Jesus, and many were filled with the Holy Ghost. Now I knew why Jesus had asked me to feed His sheep.

Soon Ben and Lanee would return to Palestine. I must have the means to feed them. "Ben, I need to know more about Jesus. Do you have scrolls that tell about Him as the rabbi did?"

"I have four scrolls. They are the accounts the disciples of Jesus gave us after He was crucified, rose again, and went back up to the Father."

"Will you let us copy them?"

"Yes, but you must begin soon. Our time is short here now."

"I'll ask Simeon and Rachel and some of their friends to

help us. Will you bring them to the meeting tomorrow?"

"Yes." Ben kept staring at me as we walked. He said, "Willem?"

"What?"

"Just how old are you?"

"Mater says I am eleven, soon to be twelve."

"Does your mater know what a keen young man you are?"

"I try not to let her in on everything I do." I smiled when I said it.

Ben shook his head and grinned too.

When we reached my insula, he did something surprising—he hugged me. Then he said, "I am so happy to have you as my friend and brother, besides my skilled interpreter. Now I need to mention that I have a feeling that we will be doing something different than going to Lanee's meeting in the next few days, like returning to the Forum to preach. Are you willing, Chezek?"

I laughed when I heard him call me Rabbi's nickname. "If Mater and Pater agree, I will do it!"

"Jesus will help us, Willem. Shalom."

"Shalom, Benjamin!"

Ben brought me two scrolls the next morning. "These are precious beyond gold. When you copy them word for word then allow others to copy yours. Perhaps Simeon could translate them into Greek or Latin, or both."

I wanted to take the scrolls directly to Simeon and Rachel, but Ben immediately asked me, "Are you allowed to help me today, Willem? The Lord *has* moved me to return to the Forum to preach. It will just be you and me for I want David and Deborah to be fresh to help Lanee with the children this afternoon."

"Pater was here late when I returned last night and I talked it over with Mater and him before he returned to the camp. They agreed I must help you for the time you have left here. The Romans who are interested in Jesus must be given an opportunity to hear about Him, as we have."

"Praise the Lord! Let's go!"

First I took the scrolls to Mater for safekeeping until I returned. She took them to the back of the cheese shop and locked them in her larger money box. Then we hurried through the city toward the Forum.

What will happen today? Every time Ben or Lanee opened their mouths in Rome something amazing happened. I could tell Ben was excited and even nervous as we made our way toward the busy Forum.

"Willem, if you feel the Holy Ghost moving on you, you must allow Him to have His way. The Lord will direct us today."

"Do you mean like he did before Rabbi prayed?"

"Yes. It could be that I am training you for the work you will do after Lanee and I return to Palestine."

"But, Ben, I'm only eleven, well, almost twelve. Could Jesus use me to preach to grown people without you?"

"He already *has* used you. *He* will be with you, dear little brother."

"I am willing."

"And that He knows."

Soon we left the wood and concrete insula-lined streets. The marble statues and buildings that surrounded the Forum rose up before us. Ben motioned me to follow and he began to hurry through the crowd down to Julius Caesar's temple. He took the steps two and three at a time. It made me think of trying to stay up with Leo. He stopped at the top of the 30 steps and waited for me. I hated that I was breathing hard when I reached him, for he didn't even seem winded.

"Hearken, citizens of Rome! Once more, it is I, Benjamin ben Jacob of Palestine, sent to bring you the good news of the coming of Jesus Christ!"

I saw the heads turn toward us, as I interpreted his words as loudly and clearly as he spoke them. Then they came running.

CHAPTER TWENTY-FOUR
PATER'S CROSS

PATER looked his men over as they stood at attention. His was a century of the elite Praetorian Guard. Many were brave soldiers who had survived battles and been given the privilege to come back to Rome to finish out their twenty-five years. Their job was to help guard the emperor and keep peace in the city.

Not that the emperor lived in Rome. *I remember the day I came back,* Pater thought. *Emperor Tiberius's barge was ahead of us taking him to the city, but for some reason he pulled to shore and turned back toward Ostia.* He resided on the island of Capri, and had never visited Rome since he left, somehow ruling Rome from the island refuge.

Years before Tiberius, Emperor Augustus had put into effect the no-marriage rule for the legionnaires. It was a dismal failure in Pater's eyes. In Gaul his superior officers had always turned a blind eye to it. Since he'd come to Rome, Pater hadn't hesitated to rotate duty schedules of others he knew were circumventing the rule, so they had every other night with their families.

But ever since the Holy Ghost had filled him at the children's meeting, Pater felt more and more uncomfortable with his lie. He definitely knew the Lord was not pleased with it. What could he do?

Pater gazed at Optio Anicia standing at attention awaiting marching orders. He wondered what *he* would do now that he had his family back together. Pater commanded the men to march, and as the sound of their hob-nailed sandals followed him, he knew he had to do something.

Leading the century through Rome, Pater remembered how the soldier had described Jesus' crucifixion. At first they made Him carry His cross until they pulled a man off the street to help Him. When they reached the site of the execution, they nailed Him to the crosspiece and pulled Him and it up to secure it to the upright. Then they nailed His feet. There He hung until He died. *I've seen men die on crosses in Gaul, but I never thought I would be in any way connected to someone who died that awful death.*

Pater led his men on to their destination near the palace. But his mind was on the picture of a man dying a slow painful death. *Jesus, you did what your Father wanted you to do, even though it was so horrific.*

That's when Pater decided. *I must marry Serena, and as soon as possible! And I must tell my superiors the truth and face the consequences.*

Never had Pater heard of anyone doing such a thing. It was a tradition that the married legionnaires lived the lie and expected everyone to look the other way.

In my heart I know the Lord can't bless my lie. What a God! He is holy and does not approve of lying. How great He is! How blessed I am to have His Spirit inside of me. I must take care to please such a one!

Pater knew he might be marching his century through the streets for the last time. He watched people scurry out of their path and noticed the pack of ragged boys running along beside them. It was a position of power he had. He had enjoyed the power. Now all he wanted was the chance to please the one who had died for him. When he turned back toward camp, Pater's focus wasn't on being a mighty Roman centurion. Rather his face was set with determination to marry Serena before the day was done—let happen what may!

How? He thought as he left the camp when his duty was over. *Does my God require something more than moving in together and proclaiming that we are married? I must find out. I will get Willem, and we will ask Ben.*

~~~

"Serena and Lucius, do you both, before God the Father, Jesus Christ the Son of God, and the Holy Ghost, pledge your true love and desire to live together for as long as you both live?"

Pater held Mater's hand with me standing behind them. We were in Ben and Lanee's room at the Lex Roma. David and Deborah each stood at my parents' sides. I interpreted, and Mater and Pater both said, "I pledge," smiling at each other. I looked at Ben who was standing in front of them.

"Do you promise to bring up Willem and any other children God may bless you with to know the Lord Jesus Christ, training them to love Him and serve Him?"

When I told them what he said, Pater and Mater turned to look at me, and both said, "I do promise."

Ben put his hand on their clasped hands and prayed, "Father, I pray you bless Lucius and Serena's marriage. Let their home be a place of refuge for the believers of Rome. Thank you for saving them, sanctifying them, and filling them with the Holy Ghost. Give them power to be a holy influence on this city and government, and let your angels protect them every step of the way, in Jesus' name, Amen." He looked up at them and with a big smile said, "Lucius and Serena, you are now before God, husband and wife."

I told them what he said then Pater hugged and kissed Mater. Turning to me, we all three hugged. Then we hugged our friends from Palestine.

Walking home through Rome's dirty streets I asked Pater, "What's going to happen now?" I was still shocked by his decision and determination not to let another day pass before he and Mater were married.

"I must report my marriage to the tribune. Then I will wait to hear what action will be taken. That's all I know, Willem. Pray for me, son. I have heard that at times some centurions have been permitted to marry under some circumstances."

Pater kissed us both when he left for camp. "I'll be back this evening if at all possible. I am so happy. No matter what happens, I am thankful the Holy Ghost showed me to make things right. Please don't worry, Serena. Our God will help us." He gave her a little hug then left.

Mater moved over to her cot, closed the curtain, and we began to get ready for bed. She said from behind the curtain, "Remember what I said about Jesus turning everything upside down? It's happening first to us, Willem." I heard the rustle of her changing out of her best tunic. Then she spoke with tears in her voice, "I thought I should never interfere with your pater's life as a soldier, but the Lord has shown him not to lie, and that we *are* his family. My thinking has been turned upside down, and tonight I am a bride!"

She stepped out from behind the curtain and lifted her hands. When she began to praise the Lord, I did too! We went on crying out our praises, until the Holy Ghost took hold of our tongues. He began to praise the Lord with words that we did not know. It was perfectus—how connected Mater and me and our God were. I felt His great love and pleasure at my pater's obedience. We were so blessed!

~~~

"Sir, I need to speak to you, if I may."

"Yes, Centurion Dio. Come in, I will be with you when I finish writing this report." He barely looked up from his work.

Pater held his helmet under his arm standing at attention.

With a sigh the officer pushed the tablets back on his desk and asked, "Now, what did you need, Lucius?"

Pater spoke again, "I have something to confess to you."

When Tribune Seneca only stared back at Pater, he continued, "I was married today. I have a common law wife and an eleven-year-old son. But just lately I have found a new faith. I have learned of the man, Jesus Christ. The Spirit of my God showed me I must not live a liar's life anymore, so I married my wife today."

Seneca's eyes widened slightly then he spoke with a rising tone, "Did your new God know that you were to remain unmarried while you served as a Roman soldier?"

A look of determination came over Pater's face. "Yes, sir. My new God knows everything, for He is our Creator. It would only please Him if I made right the lie I had been living for so long."

Tribune Seneca's face changed to a disgusted frown. "I know your time is short before you retire, Dio. What would you like to do, retire today?" He narrowed his eyes and stared up at Pater.

"Sir, I would like to continue my service until my time is up, but I submit to your judgment. My wife owns a cheese shop where I can help her, but I enjoy leading my men. I have heard that some centurions have been allowed to marry in some of the provinces."

"This is Rome, man!" Tribune Seneca snorted out. "Couldn't you have waited the few more months you had?"

"I could not after I met my God, sir. He would not allow it."

"AND WHAT ELSE WILL YOUR NEW GOD NOT ALLOW?"

Pater heard his officer's raised voice and prayed, *Jesus, help me.* Then he said, "Sir, I do not know. I have just been drawn to serve Him in the last week, and I am ignorant of many of His ways."

Seneca, the ever professional Roman tribune, took a few deep breaths and said, "Dio, you have been a mighty soldier up to now. You have fought in many campaigns and have been decorated for your valor. The position you hold in the camp is a plum your commanding general in Gaul asked that you be given. I will ask our praefect about this marriage problem. Until then I ask you to step down from your duty and leave your optio in charge of the century. For now, you are dismissed."

"Sir, may I leave the camp and be with my family until the decision is made?"

Tribune Seneca stood up. "Centurion Dio, you may become a big problem to me. But I do understand more than you think. We all wish the rule against our marrying would be rescinded. Yet as most never let their private affairs be officially known, we aren't required to deal with the infraction of the rule. But with you, we have a problem. Leave word with your optio where you will be."

"Yes, sir. Thank you."

~~~

"Did you hear that my centurion and Willem's mater got married, Lira?" Marcus said. They were sitting on a marble bench just outside the city. They had taken a stroll down the Via Appia.

"Yes. David told me they did last night. You know, Marcus, before I came to Rome, I didn't know you soldiers weren't allowed to marry. You married me."

Marcus ducked his head, and said, "I wasn't honest with you then, Lira. I am sorry for the pain you suffered when I didn't return for you. Many soldiers are guilty of the same sin. They are willing to go from post to post finding a different wife at each one." Then he lifted his head and studied her eyes. "I can say this, my Lira. I never took another woman, and I never forgot you."

Lira reached out her hand and lovingly brushed back his curly hair. She saw the sorrow in his eyes. She thought, *I won't allow anything to spoil the joy that you have given me, my Lord. Oh, after all these years I'm sitting beside my Marcus!*

"Now that Lucius has reported his marriage to our

tribune, I am in charge of the century until our officers decide what to do with him."

"But, Marcus, we are also married."

"And I am saved by the same Lord that he is."

"What will you do, my husband?"

"I told Lucius that I would also report to our tribune. But he asked me to wait until it is decided what they will do with him. Perhaps the decision will be lenient and I will be in a better position when I confess my marriage. And also the added confession could make it harder for them to be lenient with Lucius."

"We must pray, Marcus. Only God can help us all."

"Yes, I know God answers prayers. I prayed not too long ago that He would let me hear His voice and that I would be able to see you again. He's answered both of those prayers for me." He smiled down into her eyes.

Then he shook his head and said, "It's possible they could give us a dishonorable discharge and withhold our pension. That is, unless the Lord helps us."

"But aren't you and Lucius both decorated soldiers?"

"Yes, and maybe they will take that into consideration when they make their decision."

"If you are discharged, Marcus, what would you like to do? Where do you want to live?"

"I would like to live with you. And I would like to live near David and Deborah. I know so little about my son. I want to be your husband and his abba for the rest of our lives."

"Could you live in Palestine? Could you come home with me?"

"If that is where you would be happy, my only true

love, I would like to live there too."

"Marcus, that would make me so happy! We have a church in Arbela. Lanee's abba started the church as our pastor. We could help in the church. Perhaps at first you could work at Yosef's inn. That's where I have been working. Yosef is a believer. We started our church by having services in his inn."

Lira's eyes opened wider and wider as her dreams came alive. "Oh, Marcus, how you and I, and Priscilla and Jonathan, will enjoy being together! I have a little cottage near the well. David lived there with me, and when he married, Deborah moved in. We can find them another home nearby, or we can find another! Oh, Marcus!"

Marcus' eyes filled with tears, "I can't believe you love me like this, Lira! I don't deserve you—but oh, how glad I am that I married you!" He took her small hand in his and said, "Let's pray. Let's pray for Jesus to cause our superior officers to turn us in the right direction. Let's ask the Holy Ghost to help us know the way God would have us to go."

CHAPTER TWENTY-FIVE

PATER'S NEW JOB

THE praefect didn't waste any time sending word to Pater to come to his office in the camp. Pater asked Mater and Willem to be praying for him, kissed them, and left for the meeting.

Pater had been up early praying already. He thought if word came right away for a meeting, it might not be good. When he entered the praefect's quarters, his tribune was there waiting. He followed him in to stand before the mighty Praefect Macro's desk.

"Centurion Dio, I have called you here because I have been informed by Tribune Seneca that you have married contrary to the rule established by Caesar Augustus. Is this true?" The praefect was immaculately dressed in a fine linen tunic covered by his breastplate. His chest was covered in decorations of honor. His sharp features and slicked-back hair gave him the appearance of an old and wily eagle.

Pater had never had an interview with him before, though he had seen him inspecting the troops. Pater gazed back into his sharp black eyes and answered, "Yes, sir."

"Please sit down, Centurion. Our records show that you have an excellent record over the last 24 years of service. You have been commended as one of your general's best soldiers before you came to Rome. I am quite impressed by this report."

"Yes, sir."

The eagle eyes studied Pater's. "Why have you done this now?"

Pater blinked, and then began. "I have become a follower of Jesus Christ. He has saved me and has filled me with the Holy Ghost. He is teaching me not to lie. He considered my having a common law wife and illegitimate son shameful and wrong. I have had to make it right. So I married my wife."

His superior waved his hand impatiently and said, "Did you know that you could have kept that private and not let it interfere with your service to Rome?"

Pater cleared his throat and spoke again, "That is how I had been living, sir. That would not have corrected the lie. I wish to be clean of the matter according to your judgment. I have served Rome with all of my heart. I had been circumventing the rule as the convention of all the legionnaires. When my God showed me I was doing wrong, I have set about to make it right with Him, and hopefully, with you."

The praefect sighed and said, "Would you like to retire?"

"No, sir. Yet I do want to live with my family when I have time off."

"Have you told other soldiers of your actions?"

"Only one—my optio."

"Centurion Dio, do you know there are many men who have common law wives in your century?"

Pater answered, "Yes, sir."

"Do you intend to tell them to break the rule openly, too?"

Pater thought then admitted, "Sir, I do not know."

"Why is that, Centurion?"

"I do not know what Jesus Christ will have me do in the future."

Praefect Macro's eagle eyes fixed on Pater's. "Very well. Here is my judgment: you have signed on with a new commander, this Jesus Christ. He is not willing for you to keep the rules of the Roman army, or more specifically to pretend to keep the rules when you are breaking them. We have no guarantee that you will not spread this *honesty* in your century. So I am writing out your discharge papers today. You will be relieved of your duties and be expected to remove your gear by tomorrow. Because of your loyalty and fine service to Rome for the last twenty-four years, I will give you the papers to receive your pension as if you had finished out the rest of your twenty-five. You are dismissed."

Pater felt tears start in his eyes the moment he realized he was out of the army. He fought them back then turned with his head up and marched out. Tribune Seneca followed him out.

The army was his life. His whole world was shifting. He felt it as he left the shady building and stepped out into the bright sunshine. His broad shoulders sagged.

"You certainly should have kept your mouth shut, Dio. But now I'll have to say, I wish it were different," his tribune said.

Pater straightened up and said, "Thank you, sir. I will miss the army and all my men."

"What will you do?"

"I don't know yet. I will help my wife in her shop, I'm sure. But, I was hoping for better news today."

"Does this Jesus mean that much to you?"

"He gave His life for me. I am grateful and blessed to have Him as my Lord."

"Be careful, Dio, whom you call Lord in Rome. There are

many who would sell the information to the emperor, and he might have you arrested."

"As you can see from what happened today, I may not be able to be careful, where Jesus is concerned."

Tribune Seneca asked him, "Where did you hear about this Jesus?"

Trying then to be careful, Pater thought a minute and said, "I heard a preacher tell about Him in the Forum. He was from Palestine where Jesus lived. He said Jesus is the Son of the true and the living God. He said He was crucified and after three days, He arose from the dead."

The tribune almost laughed. "Did you believe that impossible report? When we Romans crucify a man, he stays dead."

"If Jesus had just been a man, He would have too, but He was God's Son, born of a virgin. He was both man and God." Pater could see the unbelief come across the tribune's face when he said it.

"If He has come back to life, where is He now?"

"The preacher said He went back up to Heaven to His Father."

That's when Tribune Seneca did laugh. "Then He's as far away as Jupiter, Apollos, and all our other gods."

Pater ignored the laughter and looked into the man's eyes. "Yes, but His Spirit is alive. He is in Rome saving the souls of men, women and children. When He saves you, you know that He is alive, and that He loves you."

With a little disgusted sound Seneca asked, "Do you know that, Dio?"

"Yes, sir. I am His servant, for He gave His life for me."

Seneca turned toward his building shaking his head. Pater went back to his room to get his belongings.

As he sorted through his clothes, he heard from behind him, "What happened, Lucius?" Pater turned to see Marcus coming through the door.

"I'm out. He did allow me my pension."

Pater felt those tears again, but turned away from his optio, throwing some clothes into a bag.

Marcus said, "I'll be right behind you, brother." And He strode out toward the tribune's room.

~~~

I saw Pater coming. He came in and dumped his bag of belongings down on the counter. We didn't have any customers at that moment. Mater came up from the back room when she saw him.

"I'm home," Pater said in a flat voice.

Mater and I both went to him and hugged him hard. Mater kept looking into his controlled face. Tears started down her cheeks. I didn't want to cry, but it was hard not to.

Pater cleared his throat then said, "Now...is there going to be a meeting at the warehouse today?"

"Yes, Pater. We were just getting ready to go."

"Well then, let me take these things upstairs, and we'll go."

We joined the stream of children heading to the meeting. When we were almost there, Lanee hurried up to us. "Willem, Lucius, and Serena, I need to speak to you before the meeting." I told Pater what she said, and he nodded. She looked excited—her eyes were shining, and her face was all lit up with a big smile.

She said, "When we get to the warehouse, stop up front with me."I told Pater what she said. We followed her in the door, and let her lead us to the corner where she could be heard over the excited children's voices.

"Willem, ask your pater if he would like to do something important for Jesus?"

I translated it to him.

"Pater said, 'since I am no longer a centurion in the Roman army, I am available to serve Him in any capacity.'"

Lanee's smile grew more brilliant. "Today," she said, "Jesus has shown me that you will be the pastor of this children's church when I leave. He wants you to begin addressing the children today so they will be prepared for my leaving. Will you do it?"

I translated her words with amazement.

Pater's eyes opened wide as he realized what she was telling him. And then I saw a gorgeous smile light up my pater's handsome face. "Yes!" he cried, and raised his muscled arm toward heaven. "I will do it, Lord, and Serena will help me!" He turned to her and saw that she too was both willing and thrilled.

I didn't need to translate that to Lanee. She saw her answer.

She opened the meeting with the words, "Today, I would like all of you to meet the one our Lord Jesus would like to help you to continue to worship Him when it's time for me to return to Palestine. He is Willem's Abba, Lucius Dio! You will call him your *pastor.* He will watch over you and help you stay strong and faithful to Jesus. Come, Pastor Dio, and greet the children!"

I told it to the children in Latin, and my pater stepped out in front of them. He was still wearing his soldier's tunic, hob-nailed sandals, and belt with his decorations.

The children became very quiet when they saw him. He spoke in a calm voice in his good Latin. "I am as surprised as you are, children. I met my one son not too long ago, and now I am given many sons and daughters to guide and love. Pray for me. And I know Jesus will help me be your good pastor."

When they realized he was finished, the children began to stand up and gather around Pater. He held out his arms and hugged them all as they came. I saw tears in his sky blue eyes.

What a wonder, Jesus! My pater is now the centurion of more than a century of little excited soldiers!

CHAPTER TWENTY-SIX

GOODBYE, ROME

THEIR faces were all aglow from the sendoff—Willem and Elise and scores of children were waving to them and crying. They watched Lucius, Serena, Rabbi Saul, and Simeon in the background; their sad smiles got smaller and smaller as they sailed on down the Tiber. What a month it had been for the two couples!

Lanee's heart was full. She watched them until the curve in the river hid them from view then she leaned over the rail and let her tears drop into the water. *Jesus, I know you'll take care of them. They're just getting started to believe in you, but I know you are not leaving them. Oh, please take care of Willem and Elise. They are so young and brave.*

Ben came up behind her and encircled her shoulders with his strong arms. "Yona, they are in the Lord's hands."

She turned in his embrace and hugged him to her. Sobbing into the smoothness of his tunic, she cried, "I love them, Ben. They will be so far away from us." When she raised her eyes, she saw tears on his cheeks. "Oh, Ben, you are crying too. Are you afraid for them?"

"They will be tried, Lanee. The Lord held His hand over us to be able to win them to Him. The faith they have is in one who turns the world upside down. But Willem and Elise are only children, as are so many we are leaving." Then he brushed his tears away with his thumbs and said, "Yet, I know Willem will be bold, for he cares about his fellow Romans.

213

Elise will follow him and help him no matter how hard it is."

"We will pray for them every day. And maybe we can return…someday." Lanee looked back through her tears in the direction of Rome.

David and Deborah came up with Marcus and Eema Lira following them. David elbowed his friend Ben and asked him, "Did you see the new harp we gave Willem when we left?"

"I did. What a great idea! He loved your music," Ben said.

"He looked so surprised and pleased!" said Deborah. "I believe he'll learn the language of the harp with the same ease as he did Hebrew."

Lanee quietly agreed, "Oh, yes…I know he'll learn to play it."

"Our wedding trip was so much better than we could even imagine back in Arbela!" David exclaimed as he hugged Deborah and Marcus to him. "Who could have guessed I'd be bringing my abba home with me? OH, THANK YOU, JESUS!"

Hearing the rejoicing in David's voice helped Lanee. She looked over at Ben and remembered his words, "They're in the Lord's hands." *How good Jesus has been to bring us all together, and how well He helped us to minister in Rome.* She felt her troubled heart relax. For it was in Jesus' strong hands she would leave Willem, Elise, and all the Roman children. She turned her eyes back down the Tiber and cried, "Goodbye, Rome! Praise the Lord for blessing you so!"

~~~

Blue watched as everyone sent Lanee and her friends off. He hid behind a stack of crates well out of sight. *The crazy people are gone—now maybe we can get back to our plan to leave Rome,* he thought. *Turk's been out of his mind, and all my frats, but soon they'll realize it was all just a wind blowing through Rome. They'll forget that Jesus. I know He's not any more real than Jupiter or Mars, or all the others.*

Blue heard Turk's whistle and realized he must have seen him. He stepped out from the crates and returned the signal.

Turk, his blond hair falling over his forehead, walked over to him, and said, "Why were you hiding?"

"I didn't want the crazy people to see me."

"I wish you wouldn't call them that. God sent them to us. They were our friends."

"And I'm your brother."

Just then they heard Willem's whistle.

"You go, Turk. I hate to hear him talk about Jesus."

"We were all friends...can't you at least talk to them?"

"I won't pretend I love a god."

"And we can't pretend we don't love our God!"

"Go, Turk! I'll see you at home later!"

CHAPTER TWENTY-SEVEN
WILLEM'S FRATERS

WAS it only a dream that I met Lanee and Ben, and David and Deborah?

But as I stroked the smooth wood of my own harp, I felt how real they had been to me.

How can I get this wonderful gift to make those pretty sounds David did? I plucked the strings softly. *I wish David were here to show me.*

I was really feeling let down. I missed my friend Ben. *It's just a week since Benjamin's Dove took them away. Did Jesus go with them?*

I carefully laid the harp on my cot and went down to the shop. Today Pater was helping Mater sell cheese.

"Willem, will you deliver this order for us? It's to the Vestal Virgins' Temple," he asked me as he set a package of cheese on the counter.

217

"Yes sir." I smiled at seeing him with only a tunic and sandals. No breastplate or hob-nailed shoes. "When I finish, Pater, may I go over to Senny's?"

"Sure, son. But don't forget the meeting this afternoon."

"Yes sir, I'll come with my fraters, if that is all right."

"Just right—I'll see you there."

After I gave Pater a hug and went to the back room to kiss Mater, I picked up the stinky package and left.

The street competed with the cheese for rankest smell. I tried to breathe through my mouth so I wouldn't have to smell either one. *Jesus, did you stay here with us, or did you leave with Lanee?* I turned aside to avoid some garbage someone probably threw out of their third floor window. *I wouldn't blame you if you did, Lord.* I remembered my dream of leaving the city. How much better *anyone's* life would be in the clean countryside.

Did you stay here with us, Jesus? Please let me know…somehow.

I took the shortcut behind the public baths to the back door of the Vestal Virgins. Draco met me in the kitchen.

"Where have you been, Willem? I haven't seen you for at least a month."

I looked into his friendly eyes, and wished I could tell him all about what I had been doing. It would be all about Jesus! Would Draco like to know about Him?

"Draco, I've been on a journey." I handed him the smelly package.

He wrinkled up his nose and took it. "Yeah? Where'd you go?"

"I went to the Great Sea first, and on the way back I met four people from Palestine." I told him about being hired to interpret for Ben, and suddenly I was telling him all about the search that I'd made for a god, and how I'd met Jesus, and about being filled with The Holy Ghost, and how the Lord had used me to help Rabbi Saul believe.

Draco's face changed as I poured all this out to him. I saw surprise, unbelief, then keen interest come into his expressive Greek eyes. When I saw the attraction, I decided to tell him who Jesus is. I told him how He died on the cross so His blood could wash away our sins and get us ready to go to Heaven when we die. Did his face ever change then! I thought his eyes might pop out of their sockets.

"Willem, are you telling me the truth? Oh, no, I know you are—you've always been honest with me. I need to meet Jesus, son. How can I do it?"

"He's in Heaven. You have to pray to Him."

"Is that what you did?"

"Yes."

"Let's do it."

"Now?"

"Show me how."

I knelt down on the tile kitchen floor, and Draco got down beside me.

"Jesus, it's me and Draco. He said he needs to meet you. Jesus, will you come and save my friend?"

I felt a little nudge inside my heart so I turned and spoke to Draco. "He wants to know if you will live for Him."

Draco nodded. "I will, if He will show me how."

"He said, if you will repent of your sins, He will wash them right away in His blood."

Then Draco turned his eyes away from me, squeezed

them shut, and began to talk to Jesus himself. "I'm so sorry I've done so many wrong things. Please forgive my sins, and wash me, dear Jesus."

Draco's eyes flew open. He cried out—"Willem, I felt them leave me! I'm so clean! Like a little baby!" Then he went down on his face, "Oh thank you, my Lord Jesus. Please teach me your ways. Thank you, thank you!"

So! I knew now that Jesus hadn't gone with Lanee—for He was right here with Draco and me. I raised my hands and began praising my Jesus. I felt tears rolling down my face, but now I wasn't ashamed to be crying in front of Draco.

He got up and began calling out, "Jesus, Jesus, oh, Jesus!"

I looked up and saw in the door of the kitchen Vestal Virgin number one— Octavia!

She pushed her matted hair off her face and slurred out, "Draco, what has gotten into you?"

Seeing her dark messy eyes full of distress, I wondered if what I had started might end in trouble.

"Why are you making this fuss?" She went up to him and took hold of his shoulder.

He didn't pay her one bit of mind. He just kept crying out, "Jesus, Jesus!"

Then I knew it was my part to explain. "May I tell you what's happened to him, Ma'am?"

She turned her eyes on me. "You're the cheese boy."

"Yes, ma'am."

Draco had gone back down on the floor and was bowing and whispering, "Jesus, thank you! Thank you!"

"Well, boy, what has happened to my usually very sensible slave?"

"He has been washed from his sins."

She pulled up the strap of her wrinkled tunic and eyed me. "His sins?"

"Yes, ma'am."

"How?"

Now I wasn't expecting this question at all. Yet I knew Jesus was giving me the open door to tell her just what I had told Draco. So again, I told about meeting Lanee and Ben and David and Deborah, about interpreting for Ben, and then about my search for the true God, and how Jesus had made Himself known to me. I saw her eyes change just like Draco's when I told her how Jesus had died and rose again. She seemed positively fascinated, so I said, "Would you like to know Jesus too?"

Octavia slid down to the floor beside Draco. "Yes...please."

I knelt beside her and prayed, "Jesus, now I am here with another friend who wants to meet you."

"It's me, Octavia. This boy has told me about you. Can you wash away my sins? All of them?"

I felt that nudge again and said, "He wants you to repent, I mean, be sorry—want to change. That way, His blood He shed on the cross will wash all your sins away."

Then she began to cry, and I really mean, cry! A big puddle of tears gathered up in front of her, and it seemed that her heart was breaking right in front of me. "I'm sorry...I'm...so...sorry," were the words I could discern between the terrible sobs.

I felt ashamed to just watch her so I looked down at the floor. Then the sobbing stopped and I heard, "Je...sus? Jesus? Did you really die for me? Will you help me get out of this mess I'm in? Oh, I believe you will...I mean I *know* you will! O thank you! Thank you!"

I noticed Draco had meanwhile finished his worship. He stood by the counter with a beautiful smile of joy on his lips. "Here's your money, *cheese-boy.* Can you bring us some more of your *sweet* cheese tomorrow?"

"I will." I smiled a big one back at him and said, "See you then."

As I walked toward Senny's, I thought, *Jesus, how did you do that? I was only there a few minutes and now two new people believe in you, and I left them rejoicing!* Seeing and smelling the same garbage didn't cause me to long for the country this trip. *It seems all different!*

Senny, Leo, and Turk, were piled up on his steps when I got there. I guess I still wore that big smile, for they all grinned back at me. I saw Blue heading our way when Leo said, "What's up, Bo?"

I told them about Draco and Octavia. They were amazed. Blue came up and sat beside Turk.

"Willem, what's our plan now?" Senny asked. "You still want to move out of Rome?"

"That's something I wanted all of us to talk about, frats. You know that Deborah paid us back for the rental of Rabbi Saul's building. Then *he* paid *her* back! Anyhow, we still have our savings."

Turk said, "What do you think Jesus wants us to do?"

"Aw, that's easy—He wants us to stay here," Senny said, "where the people are! Don't you think so, Willem?"

"It looks like it after what happened at Vestal Virgins."

Leo said, "I wish we could at least *buy* our place in the

country. Yet if Jesus doesn't want us to, I'd rather not. He is better than anything!"

"I'm so glad you said it, Leo. How is it with the rest of you? Does Jesus have first place with you?"

Blue hadn't said a word before. Suddenly he stood up and yelled, "Is that all any of you can talk about? I'm sick of hearing about Jesus. We had a great plan. We were saving up our money for it! I want to finish our plan—I want to leave Rome!"

"Why are you so angry with us, Blue? What did Jesus do to make you so mad at Him?"

"First of all, He's just like all the gods of Rome—not real. And all of you frats believing in Him has robbed me of both my brother and my friends! I hate Him!"

We all sat stunned. Blue started crying, and we didn't want to watch him.

Turk said, "You've never given Jesus a chance. Ever since you prayed to the gods to save Pater and they didn't, you've hated them."

"Shut up, Turk!"

We all waited to see what would happen next. I felt a nudge in my mind, so I said, "Would you like your part of the money, Blue? We can't plan to leave Rome. And it is your money too."

"Yes," he said.

"All right. In fact I feel like the Lord would like me to divide the money up five ways. Meet me here tomorrow, and we'll each get our part."

Blue got up and walked away.

Then Senny said, "Before you got here, Willem, we were

talking about the scrolls David and Ben had. Did you make copies? What did they say?"

"Yes, we copied them, and I have them. Would you like to hear them?"

"If they tell more about Jesus, we would!" Turk said.

"Oh, so much more. We will begin tomorrow, fraters. This afternoon, Pater said for us to come to the meeting. Do you want to see if we can find some new children for it now?"

"We haven't been to the insula next to the Via Appia yet," Leo said.

Senny stood up and turned toward the door, "I'll go tell Mater where I'm headed."

As we ambled down the dirty Roman street, I thought, *You're stuck with us now, Old Ugly, and you'll never be the same! Jesus has come to town! And Jesus, I will believe in you for Blue!*

A.D. 37

CHAPTER TWENTY-EIGHT
THE WARNING

I BLEW on my hands before I picked up my harp and walked down the steps of Julius Caesar's temple. It was after my morning message. I had sung and preached there so many times since Ben and Lanee had gone back to Palestine.

All of us had worked hard right after they left. We scoured the city and brought in many new children and parents to our gatherings at the warehouse. As time passed, Turk found a job in a bread shop nearby to help support his family. Senny began making sandals in his uncle's workshop, and Leo was apprenticed to a barber, bringing home denarii to help his large family by cutting wealthy Romans' hair. Blue had found new friends, and I didn't see him much. Turk said he had a job down at the docks.

I wasn't sure what *I* should do then. I had made some progress on my harp, and could play the song that David and Deborah had first sung in the Forum. The strings were beginning to make sense to me. Yet I would never be able to sing like they could. I missed the singing, and I missed interpreting Ben's preaching. One sleepless night, flipping and flopping around on my cot, I finally did some thinking about the future instead of looking back.

I realized I didn't like living in Rome any more than I used to, but I saw that I had begun to love the people of Rome— I cared what happened to them. Then it just came to me to ask Jesus a question.

Lord, why did you show me to Lanee before she came? Who am I? Why did you pick me out of all the boys in Rome? I listened with my heart all open for Jesus to speak.

I added, *Ben said I would preach for you.* I felt Jesus was listening.

Then I heard Him say, *Do you want to preach for me?*

"Yes, Lord!" I said out loud then remembered that I might wake up Pater and Mater on the other side of the room behind their curtain.

Yes, I do, Lord. I loved interpreting for Ben. I never knew what he was going to say, and everything he said was exciting to hear. If I did preach, would it be that good?

It would be, was His answer.

When? Where? I asked.

Then something Pater said after Ben left came back to my mind. He said the people were still gathering at Caesar's statue, looking for Ben to come back. I remembered the maters running with their children, the slaves grabbing their shopping bags and hurrying toward us, and the nobles and businessmen gathering. Then the awesome sight of the Romans kneeling on the pavement formed in my mind.

The Forum?

The next morning I set out on my own with my harp in my hand. I didn't have David and Deborah to sing for me. But I could sing (a little), and I could speak Latin and Greek. And I did have the Holy Ghost. When I got to Julius Caesar's determined-looking form, a woman recognized me and cried out. Soon a small crowd was gathered.

I was too shy to try singing, but I lifted my voice and said,

"Benjamin has gone back to Palestine. But Jesus has sent me to preach to you. He has raised me up, a boy in Rome, to tell you of His great salvation! You have sought the help of the gods of marble all glorified in your Forum and found no help. Finally the true and living God has come to help you." I took a deep breath and cried out as I knew Ben would, "His name is Jesus Christ. He grew up a man in Palestine. His Father is the God that you have needed. If you will believe in His Son, Jesus Christ, He will wash all your sins away in Jesus' precious blood and save your soul!" I scanned their upturned faces and asked, "Will you believe? If you repent of your sins, He will accept you, and you will be His child from now on."

Their faces told me they did believe. When I came down the steps, they surrounded me. I said, "We have a place where we that believe in Jesus meet." Then I told them about the warehouse and when to come.

It wasn't hard. The way had already been made easy for me by my wonderful friend Benjamin ben Jacob. *Thank you, Jesus!*

That was a little over three years ago. Since then I've been able to add music to my message. There came a day when I understood the mystery of the harp. Then I began to understand how to piece a song together. Now I have many songs that I can play and sing when I preach.

I'd just finished my message to a large crowd. Some of them were from our church, but many, especially slaves and nobles, I only saw here week after week. They brought friends, and at times I could tell the nobles were doing it as a form of amusement. Some days soldiers came and listened.

But every time I preached, Jesus let me enjoy what I told them just like He said! I loved to preach!

I shivered a little then headed toward home. It had turned quite cold in the night, and I had worn a woolen cloak. The street was crowded as I passed out of the Forum and I felt a shoulder jostle me. When I heard the stifled cough, I turned and saw it was Nicholas beside me!

He smiled into my eyes. "It's been a long time since I've seen you, Willem. You've grown!" he said.

I smiled back and said, "Yes, sir. I just turned fifteen." I wondered how the old man had just popped up beside me on the crowded street. I slowed down to walk with him.

"As you can see old Nicholas is still alive, though sometimes my breathing is much worse than today." He turned his head and coughed. I walked slower. It was really good to see him again!

"Are you still looking for abalone shells?" I asked. "I've not been back to the Great Sea to find any more."

He stared at me then looked ahead as we walked. "That's too bad. Those I bought from you were excellent specimens... no, I didn't look you up for abalone shells today. Rather I've come because of your new profession—the preaching in the Forum, and I understand, other places round about Rome."

"Have you heard me, sir? Have you heard about Jesus Christ?"

"I heard a little of your message today. But I didn't come to the Forum to hear about Him. I came to warn you." He turned his head and hacked several times. "A report has been sent to Tiberius concerning you and the growing sect you and your pater have started. He has sent word from Capri that you are to be arrested and sent to him, along with your pater."

The news startled and excited me!

Nicholas studied my face then continued, "I heard of it, and decided to give you warning hopefully in time for you to escape."

I wasn't sure what caused my voice to tremble when I said, "We won't try to escape. I have to talk to Pater, but I don't think we will."

"Tiberius is not rational, boy! If you fall into his hands, you may be lost. Your pater *is* a rational man. Surely he will know what to do. I believe from what I've been told, if you preach in the Forum tomorrow, you will be arrested. So take heed."

I stared at the backs of the people walking in front of us, and said, "Thank you, Nicholas."

But when I turned, he was gone. So I sped down the crowded streets to Pater. I knew he was working at the church. *The church—it's what Jesus called us believers in Matthew's scroll.* As I neared the warehouse which we now called the church, I thought of how it looked when Ben and I first saw it. Pater and all the parents had worked a miracle on the old rough building.

I ran into the door and found Pater on the entrance floor setting mosaic tiles.

"What's your hurry, son? Something wrong?"

"I—I think so." I moved over to the bench beside the door, carefully laid my harp down, and shrugged off my cloak. "Pater, do you remember Nicholas from the army camp?"

Pater laid another piece of tile and without looking up, said, "Yes. He outfitted all the men with whatever gear they needed. I didn't get to know him too well before I left."

I squatted down beside him. "I sold him some abalone shells right about the time you came home. I met him on the street just after my message in the Forum today. He showed up right beside me as I walked home. Pater...he said he came to warn me."

Pater laid his trowel down. He got up and reached for my hand to pull me up. When he looked me in the eyes, I felt the first little prickle of real fear start creeping up my spine. "What did Nicholas tell you, son?"

"The emperor knows about my preaching. I will be arrested tomorrow. And Pater, you will be too."

My pater swallowed then I saw his face change from his gentle pastor's face to the face of the hardened soldier I'd first seen. "He knows that for sure, son?"

"Yes, sir. He wanted us to run."

"What did you tell him, Willem?"

"I told him I didn't think we'd run, but I had to talk to you."

Pater took a deep breath then sighed. "We need to pray. Help me clean all this up and we'll go home to Mater. She'll help us pray."

We put all his tools and tile away then bundled up in our cloaks and headed home. When we told Mater, she cried out. Then with tears glistening in her eyes, she closed the shop. We all knelt on the floor of our apartment upstairs and began to seek Jesus.

"What do you want us to do, dear Savior?" Pater prayed.

Mater really cried then, and whispered, "Lord, our family

has been together only for such a short time. Please protect us. Yet, I know you died for us."

As I knelt, I felt the streak of excitement return. I wanted to go. I wanted to see the palace. I knew Tiberius was on the island of Capri. I wanted to see him. I wanted to talk to him about Jesus!

Pater stopped praying with an awed expression. "God just showed me that you are to make the decision, Willem."

I remember when I wanted to go to the Great Sea. How horrified Mater was when she knew I'd gone. Now, how could I tell her?

"Lucius, are you sure God showed you that? Willem has barely turned fifteen. He's too young to know how dangerous it would be. Surely the best thing would be for us to leave Rome…"

Pater raised his hand, and Mater didn't finish.

I had to speak. I had to tell it just like I felt it. "I want to go! I can't think of anything I'd rather do! Oh, Mater, I could tell Emperor Tiberius about our real God, and the best friend anyone could ever have—our Lord Jesus! Mater, wouldn't Jesus protect us? He's greater than the emperor!"

Mater looked at me with such a shocked expression. "He's a mad man, Willem! Remember how he turned on his Praefect Sejanus, and how he had him and his whole family murdered!"

Pater said, "Did Jesus tell you He wants us to go, Willem?"

"No, sir. But when I started to pray, suddenly the excitement of going got hold of me. It felt like it does just before I open my mouth for Jesus in the Forum. I love it! I'm not afraid. It will be perfectus!"

Pater bent back over the floor, so Mater and I did. He began, "Lord, you have given Willem joy and excitement in place of fear about being arrested tomorrow. We thank you for it. Now I ask you to touch Serena and me that we will see it the same way."

Mater whispered, "I ask you to make a way for me to go, too. I can't wait here not knowing what will become of mine, Lord."

When we got up, Pater went to Rabbi Saul's and told him what was happening—they would know what to do with the church and the shop if we didn't return. I ran over through the cold to Senny's. My frats needed to know, so they could pray for us. I told him, and made sure he knew I *wanted* to go. And I asked him to tell the others, especially that part. He tried to get me to wait for all of them to gather, but I said no, it would be hard for me. He said he'd tell them, and as I left he grabbed me and hugged me.

"I'll be back, Senny!" I yelled over my shoulder as I ran through the cold air.

I had just about made it home, when she saw me. Who else? Elise. Ever since we had helped Lanee and Ben together, all she wanted to do was be my constant companion! I did not want to tell her anything about this.

"Willem, where are you headed in such a hurry?"

"I have to get home, Elise." I kept on walking…fast!

"Why?" She moved up beside me and walked fast too.

"I can't tell you." I wouldn't look at her. Those brown eyes would get me.

"WAIT!" She commanded.

I stopped and stared into her smoldering eyes. "What?"

"You are in some adventure, and you're going to keep me out of it! I know you Willem! Tell me what it is!"

"You will cry if I tell you, and I don't want to see you cry."

And guess what she did? She started crying!

"You...you...meany...you...you... are meaner to me than you are to anyone else...and...I...I...like you!"

Then she hid her face.

Now I wanted to hide mine. *She likes me? Elise likes me?* I started to yell at her, *Well, I sure don't like you!* when I felt Jesus touch my heart very gently. *All right, Lord.*

The street was mostly empty because of the cold. I grabbed her by the hand and guided her to the curb. Even though I was shivering, I got her to sit down with me.

I let go of her hand and said, "Elise, I'm going to tell you what is happening, but you mustn't do anything else about it but pray. Will you promise?"

She dried her eyes on her red wool sleeve, and nodded, looking a little ashamed of herself.

"Tomorrow when I go to preach in the Forum, my pater and I will be arrested and taken before Emperor Tiberius. My mater plans to go, too."

Her eyes got bigger. She swallowed what I thought was a sob then she said, "I must go, too."

How did I know she was going to say that?

"No. You cannot. But, Elise, I need you to pray for us. Here. And I need you to get the other children to pray for us. Will you do it?"

"I...guess so. But can't I go, too?"

"No."

She stared into my eyes and reached for my hand. *Jesus,*

if you hadn't touched me, I would not put up with this.

"Willem, are you afraid?" she finally asked.

"Sometimes...but mostly I'm excited!"

I saw her look at me with all I could say was *admiration.* It made me want to bark at her to stop it!

"Willem...before you go...will you let me...hug you?"

"Why?" Those brown eyes looked ready to cry again, so I put my arm around her scrawny neck, and pulled her to me. I laid my head on her fuzzy hair like Mater did mine then I pulled away. "Will that do?"

She smiled into my eyes, and something hit me.

She's not so bad!

I stood and helped her up onto her feet. I don't know why but I held her cold hand until we stopped in front of her stoop. "Remember to pray, Elise."

"I'd rather go with you."

"Next time I'll take you."

"I won't forget you said that, Willem."

"I know."

~~~

We didn't get much sleep that night. Early in the morning Mater sent Pater and me to the baths. She had gone the night before when Pater visited Rabbi Saul. We put on our best clean clothes and warmest cloaks and ate as much as we could hold for breakfast.

When we entered the Forum a crowd was already gathering near Julius Caesar for my early message. We three climbed the stairs and turned toward the crowd, that's when we heard the soldiers' hob-nails heading in our direction. I raised my hands, looked to the heavens, and breathed out, "Oh, thank you, Jesus!"

CHAPTER TWENTY-NINE

UNDER ARREST

THE Praetorian Guard didn't know what to do with Mater at first. She took hold of both of our arms and wouldn't let go! The soldiers were very polite to Pater, and didn't question him about Mater as they marched us out of the Forum.

At first the crowd watched in silence, then one voice shot out of the middle, "Where are you taking them?"

The centurion answered, "They are ordered into a hearing with the emperor."

They all scattered when they heard that. Mater's hand squeezed my arm; she was determined to go along.

The frowning centurion spoke to Pater, "Dio, we have no accommodations for a woman. She was not ordered to appear before Tiberius."

Pater spoke up to the man, "She is my wife and the boy's mother. I choose not to leave her behind. I will guard her. We are going peacefully and will cause you no trouble."

"Very well, at your word I will allow it. I have heard much of your valor and decorations in the service of Rome, sir. My men have been your men in the past, and they do not forget you."

"And I will not forget your kindness toward me and my family, Centurion."

We spent that day and night in a locked room of the Praetorian Camp. There were only two cots in the room. They had lit a fire in the brazier which gave us some comfort. Late that night the stout iron door was unbarred, and a soldier appeared with another cot. Behind him I heard Nicholas announcing himself with a short coughing spell.

He came in looking sorrowful. "I had hoped to prevent this by warning you, Willem!" he said as he shrugged off his woolen cloak.

Pater got up from the cot and answered him. "Thank you very much for warning us, sir. I am Willem's pater, Lucius Dio, and this is his mater, Serena. Your warning allowed us to make some much-needed preparations before we were arrested." He smiled into Nicholas' worried eyes.

"Yes, Dio. I remember seeing you back when you arrived in the camp." He coughed and then said, "You are quite cheerful, I see. I won't try to dampen your cheer, though I can't feel it in this situation myself."

"We are only here because we preach and trust in Jesus Christ. We have done no wrong," Mater said. "Have you heard of Him?"

"Yes, dear lady. Yesterday before I warned Willem, I listened to his sermon. He said Jesus was crucified for me. I have thought much about it since I heard the strange thing. Why would your beliefs be based on such a statement?"

"It is true," I said.

"That's why it has stuck in my craw. I know you. I know you are a boy who is both intelligent and honest. Why would Jesus die on a cross for me, if He did for anyone? I have never heard of Him before. Did He know me? How could I have been important to Him? And then you said He arose from the dead. Alive again, eh? Does that mean He is interested in me now?"

Pater said, "If the true *Son of God* were crucified, He could know you and care about you as He died, and as He lives now."

Nicholas nodded and coughed into his arm, and said, "You speak as if there were only *one* God. Do you not believe in Jupiter and all his cohorts?"

I said, "I do not believe in them, because they are not real."

"As I also have decided, Willem. But now you truly believe in your one God. What is His name?"

"He is called Jehovah in the Jewish writings. But we know Him as the Father of our Lord Jesus Christ."

Nicholas thought on that a minute then asked, "How did you come to believe in Him?"

Then I told him the whole story of Lanee and Ben being sent to Rome by Jesus. Also I told him that before they came, Jesus had showed me to Lanee. Then I said, "When I began to pray to Him, He began to answer my prayers, and even talk to me. He will do the same for you, if you will repent of your sins and believe enough to ask. He was no sinner, yet He knows that we are full of sin. His sinless blood was shed to wash our sins away. He wants you to open your heart to His mercy, so you can go be with Him and His Father when you die, Nicholas."

He studied my face in the dim lamp-light. A spasm of coughing caused him to look away. Recovering he said, "Tonight I will think about these things." He picked up a bundle and went to Mater. "Before I go, I wanted to offer you these linens for your sleep tonight, dear mother of my young friend. I would like for you to carry them with you on the ship and use them as long as you should need them."

He gave Mater a large rolled-up blanket tied around with a scarlet cord.

"Goodbye. I hope you will return to Rome with the emperor's blessing!" When he said this, he peered at us with a bitter haggard look. I knew he doubted that could ever happen. Then he recovered his cloak and slipped out of the door.

We heard the bar being slid back in place. "Let's pray for him, Pater!"

Kneeling on the rough tile, we cried out to Jesus for Nicholas. The Holy Ghost began praying through us all. Our praying had a mournful and sweet sound. Hearing it told me that Nicholas was loved in Heaven.

Later when Mater untied the scarlet cord and unrolled the dark grey blanket, she gasped! A down-filled pillow tumbled out, and a couple of sheets of the softest linen. Among the sheets were a jar of sweet-smelling oil, a comb, and a soft grey tunic and stola.

Pater patted her on the arm, and said, "It seems Jesus is pleased that you are accompanying us, Serena!"

"Lucius, all of this is nicer than any I have ever seen! Where did Nicholas get such finery?"

"Mater, you should see his place at the camp! He is a collector of fine things. Surely when He sees the worth of Jesus, he will want Him as his own!"

We all laughed for joy at the thought. Almost at once we all grew quiet. The same thought probably went through all our minds—how worried Nicholas looked.

Mater sighed a long trembling sigh and said, "I'd almost forgotten why we are here."

Pater replied, "Tiberius loves the army, Serena. I believe he will take my service into account."

"Maybe we should pray again," I said.

As we got back down on our knees, I cried out, *Jesus, just don't let us be afraid. We can face anything. Just don't let us be afraid!*

Mater and Pater held each other, and I glanced at their clasped hands. Pater's was steady on Mater's shaky hand. I felt the Holy Ghost touch my heart, and I spoke out, "Fear not! Greater are those that are for thee, than those that are against thee!"

Pater let go of Mater and lifted his hands with praise. Then we all did. That's when the Holy Ghost came down in the cell and spoke through us! Though I didn't understand the words, I knew He was glorifying Jesus and God the Father! We just let Him have His way it seemed for hours. When the Spirit would die down a moment, one of us would cry out again to the Lord for His comfort and assurance, and again the Holy Ghost would fall upon us.

Finally we lay down to sleep. Pater said in a quiet voice, "Willem, I want to thank you for being so brave about this. I have faced many battles before, but you are just a boy. You are leading your mother and me into trusting the power of the Lord. Thank you, son."

"That also goes for me, Willem," Mater said in her sleepy voice.

I blew out the lamp and tried to get comfortable on the cot with the rough army blanket over me. Soon I heard my parents' regular breathing and knew I was alone in the night. I could dimly make out the rafters above me as my eyes adjusted to the darkness.

Lying quietly for the first time in hours, it seemed I began dreaming with my eyes open. The rafters seemed to change into a cross with a man hanging on it. It had to be Jesus! I knew He was dying for me. His blood was leaving His body great drops at a time. I was underneath those drops. I felt them on my face and hands. I felt them roll down into my ears, and over my chest. I lay there crying as softly as I could. Then my heart spoke to Him, *It is enough, Jesus. It is enough for me.*

CHAPTER THIRTY

THE EMPEROR'S SAVIOUR

IT was early when they marched us to the Tiber. Ten soldiers hurried us through the cold deserted streets. As we neared the docks, I suddenly saw Leo running back toward our insulas.

"Pater…did you see Leo?" I whispered.

"Yes. He'll tell everyone what's happening to us. That's good."

We were led onto a barge similar to the one I saw Pater on that day, only smaller. Along with us and five of the soldiers, clay jars and wooden crates were evenly distributed about the barge. We sat on the crates.

A sharp "Whee!" split the air. It was Senny's whistle. I spotted my fraters jumping down from the dock to the sand at the bow of the barge.

I asked the soldier near me as I motioned toward them, "Could I speak to my friends before we go?"

He shrugged his shoulders, so I went quickly to the bow, "Frats! I'm glad to see you!"

"I was on the lookout, Bo!"

"Yes, I saw you running."

"Wish we could go too," Turk said. "You're going to see that ugly old man, and tell him about Jesus?"

"Yes, and I'm looking forward to it." I grinned at them, and they laughed. "Still, you'd better pray for us. Some say he's not sane."

"We'll make sure the others know you're leaving today," Leo said.

Looking toward Senny, I said, "Take charge for me." Then I added, "But don't worry, I shall return!"

The soldier took my arm and led me back to my seat.

"Willem!" When I turned back I saw them all smiling at me.

"Twee!" I whistled softly as I sat down by Pater. Then I heard all of their whistles sound off as they moved away. Pater placed his arm over my shoulder. His other arm was protectively draped over Mater's.

Something made me look back where my frats had been standing. One of them was still there. I thought they'd all left.

No, it was Blue.

I motioned to him, and asked the soldier could I go speak to him. He nodded. I hadn't seen Blue for months. He had grown taller. His blue eyes seemed bluer and his red hair bushed out all over his head.

"Blue!" I said, and couldn't help smiling my heart.

"Willem. Turk told me you were arrested. You're sailing to meet that old crazy man Tiberius!"

"Yes, Blue. Don't you wish you could go with me?"

"I knew you used to want to leave Rome, but I don't think this is what you hoped for."

"Well, I feel different now. I'm going for Jesus...oops... I guess you still hate Him."

"Who is there to hate?"

"Hey, Blue! What do you think Tiberius will do to me and my family?"

"He's been known to throw people off the cliff into the sea. Aren't you worried, Willem?"

"Sounds like you're worried."

"I don't want you to die."

"Blue, what if I make it back here? What if I return and am still allowed to preach in Rome? Would you believe in Jesus then? Would you be willing to believe He's different than the other gods of Rome?"

"It's not going to happen, Willem, though I hate to say it."

"What if it does?"

"All right, if you come back and preach in the Forum again—you and your parents—I'll have to believe that Jesus is a different kind of god. And, Willem, I dearly hope he is, for your sake!"

Just then the soldier came and got me. I smiled back at Blue, and gave a little "Twee!"

I heard his answer behind me. When I turned to sit down, he was gone.

The captain of the barge got the vessel under way toward Ostia. As we moved down the Tiber, I talked to Jesus. *Will you take care of my fraters while I'm gone? I know this sounds strange coming from me, Lord, but will you bring us safely back to Rome? Back to our work for you? And Lord, will you take care of that little girl, Elise?*

~~~

When we reached Ostia, we were hurried to a sailing ship headed for the island of Capri. It was the first time I'd ever been out on the Great Sea, and Mater and I got seasick. I began to feel better after about 2 hours, but Mater was still very sick. She and Pater were below on a bench in the cabin. She lay with her head in his lap, until she had to run to the rail again. I prayed she could get better like I had.

The soldiers let me explore the ship. It was cold outside of the cabin, but my woolen cloak helped. I heard the sailors say we were having a favorable wind, and should be there after midnight. They offered me some food, but I still didn't feel like eating.

I went below to tell Pater what they'd said about arriving.

"Son, sit down and let's talk before we get to Capri," he said as he lightly smoothed Mater's brow. "I don't know if Tiberius will let us stay together once we are there. If something happens and we are separated, I want you to blow your frat-whistle every now and then. I will answer if I can with my own. It will sound like this, "Tawheet!" If you hear mine, try to answer me."

"Pater, will Mater be all right?"

"As soon as she steps foot off this ship onto dry land, the sickness will leave her. Don't worry."

I said, "My stomach is better, but I'll be glad to get back on land."

"I was only seasick once. After that it never bothered me again. Maybe that's how it will be with you."

We sat for awhile with our own thoughts then I remembered what I'd heard about Tiberius. I asked, "Do you think the emperor is insane?"

"If he thought it would benefit him to be thought insane, then yes, he could act the part. No man could run this vast empire with such success and not have good sense."

Then I asked, "Why do you think he wants to see us?" The question had come to me over and over.

"I...uh...don't know, son."

"Pater, will you give me your opinion, even if it isn't good? I think I need to know."

"You are young, Willem. Rome is sometimes cruel to its citizens, especially those who try to make changes."

"So, you believe he may want to harm us. Would Jesus let him do that, Pater?"

"It seems the Lord has given you a great desire to see Tiberius. That makes me think that he won't be able to do us any harm. I do not believe we are heading to our death. The emperor may command us not to preach Jesus anymore in Rome. That would be very difficult to obey, wouldn't it?"

"Yes, sir. I have thought that. Yet, I have also hoped that Jesus will completely win him over! Wouldn't that be a grand thing?"

Mater lifted her head a little and said hoarsely, "My son the dreamer!"

"Mater, I have seen Him save a vestal virgin and her slave. I have seen Him completely change a decorated Roman centurion. I have heard His voice and been shown His love. It wasn't just a dream. Why should I doubt He could save Tiberius?"

"Then you are the right one to tell him, Willem!" Pater said.

I didn't sleep until we arrived at the island late that night. The wind was up and we all felt it through our cloaks. The island seemed surrounded with white cliffs, but soon we saw a break—it was a rocky beach. The ship let us out in a small rowboat with our guard. There was a light there, and some soldiers were waiting by a guardhouse for us. As I left the rowboat, I whispered, "Help me, Holy Ghost!" when I thought of the task that lay before me.

The guard opened the door of the small building and motioned us inside. We heard him lock us in. No cots or chairs of any kind were in the room, so we all got into Mater's bedroll on the floor. We snuggled up and began to warm up.

"I'm a lot better," Mater whispered.

"I'm glad, Mater," I whispered back then said, "I am so hungry!"

That's when Pater got up and banged on the door. When the guard came, he asked if we could have some food. After awhile, the soldier brought us a plate of some kind of meat, a loaf of black bread, and a jug of water. When we tasted the meat, we decided it was pork. We ate every bit they gave us, for even Mater found she was hungry.

Finally we could rest. I could hear the waves sounding far

away. The swooshing sound soothed me to sleep. I remember hearing Pater sleepily utter a prayer, "Thank you, Jesus, for bringing us safely here. We are in your hands."

That night I dreamed...*Oh, no, there's a fire! It's burning ever closer to the people. That little boy is clinging with terror to his mother. The fire is burning so close to them, it has suddenly caught his mother's dress on fire and her hair is singed!*

I watched the dream change...*The little boy, it's him all right, but he's grown. He's holding a sword and his hands are stained with blood. He is the victor in the battle, and he raises the sword in celebration, but as he lowers it, that same frightened look crosses his strong young face.*

Again the dream changed...*Oh, the boy is old and sick. His mouth is twisted in a cruel grin, and he's watching while his soldiers kill helpless men, women, and little children. He's glad they're dead! But then the satisfied expression fades and becomes the terrified expression of the little boy. He hides his head in his hands and weeps.*

I awoke and looked around me. Mater and Pater were both already up. He was trying to straighten his crumpled clothes. I saw she had changed into the tunic and stola Nicholas had given her. I put on my sandals and let Mater pull the comb through my hair. The dream had left me groggy and unhappy. It was a nightmare. But I knew who that little boy was.

"Willem, remember what I told you last night," Pater said.

"Yes, sir. I hope they don't separate us, though."

Just then the door was unbolted and the soldiers hurried us out into the blinding sunlight.

"The emperor wants to see you as soon as we can get

you up to the villa," the centurion told Pater.

He let us stop at the latrine then marched us up the trail. The wind wasn't as cold as last night and the sun warmed us as we walked. The trail wound around and around gradually bringing us to the hilltop where the palace of Tiberius was perched. The soldier told us the palace was called the Villa Jovis.

He led us through the guarded gate and to a row of rooms just inside the wall. Pater nodded to me when they began to place us in separate rooms.

I found a tub of bath water, soap, and clean clothes in mine. There were even cloth shoes I supposed I was to wear in the palace. I bathed and dressed then waited. I kept seeing the boy's frightened face in my mind. I knew it was Tiberius, for I remembered him on the barge. Why had I dreamed of him?

"Tawheet!" Pater signaled. I heard another two notes— "peep-peep!" and answered them both. I breathed a sigh of relief. *So far, everything is all right.*

I sat on a chair beside the bed, wondering what would happen next.

After a long wait there came a knock on the door, which immediately opened before I could answer it. A brawny servant brought in a tray of food and drink. He looked me over before he set the tray down.

"You must eat and then be ready for your audience with the emperor," he said.

The man stood over me like he was going to watch me eat.

"Will I be accompanied with my pater and mater?" I asked as I lifted the cover off the tray.

"They are with him now. When they return, you will be called." He picked up my dirty clothes and sandals, and looking satisfied that I was eating, he started toward the door.

"Thank you," I said as he turned to leave.

Then he looked back and said, "Be careful what you say. He is not a happy man."

"Why do you warn me?"

He lowered his voice and said, "You and your parents are not criminals. I know that you are here for preaching Jesus in Rome. I have heard about Him from one who heard the young Jew preach in the Forum a few years ago. My friend is a follower of Jesus."

I felt the Holy Ghost leading and asked, "But you do not follow Him?"

He turned away from me and said, "I…I am a slave. I have not felt worthy of such a person." He set my dirty clothes back on the floor and began to straighten my bed.

I chewed up the bite of bread I'd taken then asked, "But… isn't your friend also a slave?"

His voice trembled a little when he answered, "Yes, but she is a beautiful woman, and would be worthy of the greatest king that ever lived."

He came and stood over me again after he'd finished with my bed. I stopped eating and said, "May I ask Jesus if He would like for you to follow Him?"

"What could I ever do for Him? I am a slave. Now you must eat, and I must watch for your parents to be brought back."

I picked up a grape and asked, "What is your name? My name is Willem."

He motioned for me to keep eating then said, "I am

Plenius. I was brought from Gaul."

I dug back into the food but said before I took the bite, "I will ask Jesus if He wants you. I will ask Him to let you know His answer."

"How? No, don't talk anymore...Willem...eat!" Then he picked up my dirty clothes again and left me alone.

I prayed as I ate, *Jesus, help Mater and Pater with Tiberius. Lord, would you show Plenius that you want him, too? I need you to go with me when he calls for me. I need you to show me what to say.* The food was strengthening me, and my prayer was delivering me from fear. *Thank you, Saviour, for your help. I love you, Jesus. I will try to help Tiberius to believe in you. I believe you love him, Lord.*

When I finished both, Plenius came for me. I heard a soft "Tawheet!" and Mater's two note whistle as I left with him. I looked at Plenius and blew my answer. He acted like he'd not heard.

We walked through a chilly marble hallway without windows. Statues of famous men or perhaps gods met us all along the way. Then we came to a doorway which opened on our right, and Plenius said, "When you approach the throne, do not bow, and do not look directly at him until he speaks to you. He may not speak for several minutes; just be still until he does."

He left me then.

I walked into the room. It was all marble and gold. A large brazier was glowing red in one corner. Through a huge glass window behind the throne the blue sea's waves rolled in toward the island. I walked in the direction of the throne, keeping my eyes on the rolling waves behind him to keep from looking directly at the emperor. A safe distance away, I stopped.

All was quiet.

Then I heard him clear his throat.

"You may look at me…Willem."

I turned my eyes on the man I'd seen on the barge near Ostia.

He was even uglier. His face was a mess of little bandages and healing sores. Large piercing eyes looked back at me. He was completely bald, and his shoulders were stooped. A dark woolen cloak partially covered up the beautiful purple tunic he had on.

I saw he wore the same circlet of gold I'd seen before I'd bowed to him that day on Julian's ship. I didn't like him. But he was also the boy in my dream.

He lifted his bulging sad eyes to mine and said, "Will you tell me of Jesus?"

It was a shock. But, remembering the boy, I said, "Yes, sir. I mean, your Highness."

"No. I do not need your homage. I need to find out what

you know about Jesus Christ."

I didn't hesitate. Remembering how I preached to the people in the Forum who had never heard about Jesus, I began, "Because God so loved the people of this world, He wanted to save them from their evil ways. He sent His Son down to live in Palestine not long ago. He sent Him to teach the people how to love God and their neighbors. His Son was Jesus Christ, whose name means the *anointed One who saves.*

"Jesus didn't just come to teach the people, He came to die for the people. Jesus was hated by the Jewish religious leaders, and they sought to kill Him. He was arrested and at the permission of Pontius Pilate was crucified." When I told this part I couldn't help feeling tears start in my eyes.

"He hung there dying, not for His own sins, for He had none. He was suffering the punishment for *our* sins on the cross. He died after six hours of torment. But because He was God's Son, He didn't stay dead. He arose from the dead on the third day. After showing Himself to His disciples and even five hundred people at once, He was taken up in a cloud to Heaven, where He sits beside God right now." I stopped.

The emperor stared into my eyes. "Has He... *saved*...you, Willem?"

"Yes, sir."

"Tell me about it."

I told about my wanting the gods of Rome to help me with a problem I had. Then I had to tell him that I decided that none of the gods were real. I wasn't sure how he would take that so I whispered to myself, *help me, Jesus.* Then I told him about Ben and Lanee coming (without mentioning their names), and how they knew me before they came to Rome, for Jesus had shown me to the girl.

"When the young Jewish man spoke in the Forum, I began to hope Jesus would love me and save me. When I prayed to Him, He answered me."

I noticed the emperor began to shake. But I kept on speaking. "Then the young Jewish woman preached to some of us children in Rome, and the Holy Ghost came down and filled us. We all began to speak in a language we never had learned. It was the sign that He had come to us. He is our Comforter, since Jesus is gone back to Heaven."

When I finished he was really shaking, almost violently enough to fall out of his throne. I felt alarmed, yet I knew his frightened expression.

"What is the matter, sir? Are you sick?"

Still shaking uncontrollably, he said, "I will soon...go and stand before...the God you are telling of, and I am guilty of...heinous evil."

It was true, how evil he was! I knew it from my dream!

Then I felt Jesus touch my heart, like He did when Elise said she liked me. I opened my mouth, "You will not go unprepared, if you so desire, my emperor."

"What did you say, boy?"

I spoke up louder. "I said, you will not go unprepared, if you so desire, sir."

He shook, and his great eyes bore into mine. "How? When?"

"Jesus Christ has paid for your evil on the cross of Calvary. And the when is now...if you so desire, sir."

Still shaking, he uttered in an urgent voice, "What shall I do? I am dying ...I know it...What shall I do to be saved?"

I answered, "You must confess your sins to Jesus, and ask His pardon. Then you must believe that He has forgiven you for them."

He held his gnarled hand out toward me. "Come here, Willem."

I walked up close to him. He looked even sicker to me there. "Will... you pray for me?" He said still trembling from head to foot.

The boy...I thought.

That's when I lifted my hand and laid it on Tiberius' head. His bald head was sweating. I remembered how Jesus had saved Draco and Octavia as I said, "You must repent of the wrong that you have done, sir. Will you do that?"

"Yes...I repent...I have no excuse for my murdering and cruelty...Jesus Christ, I repent!" he cried fearfully. "Please forgive me!"

I didn't like being so close to Tiberius. He was so ugly and I knew he was cruel. But I knew Jesus loved him. "Oh, Jesus, will you forgive him? Help my emperor to be ready to meet you! Surely you died for him. You bore the punishment for all his sins. Help him, Jesus, to know you love him."

What I noticed first was his shaking stopped. I opened my eyes and met his. They were looking at me, then inwards, then back at me again.

He drew in a long breath, closed his eyes and sighed it out. Then he said, "You may go, Willem. I will call for your pater again, but then I will allow you all to return to Rome."

He looked inward again then said, "I ask that you remember me when you hear that I have died. Others will rejoice at my death for all my wickedness, but remember how you helped me prepare."

"Sir? Are you saved? Did Jesus wash away your sins in His blood?"

"I am saved. I am cleansed from all my wretched sins in the blood of Jesus, the Son of God!" he said with a weak smile. "Let Him be praised!"

CHAPTER THIRTY-ONE

THE JOURNEY HOME

I WAS escorted back to my room by Plenius. How he knew to come for me at the last word the emperor spoke, I did not know. He smiled at me as we walked back down the long marble hall and said, "Now I know Jesus wants me."

"But, how?"

"I was listening."

"You heard the emperor get saved?"

"Yes. I have often thought that the only person it would be harder for Jesus to want than me would be my master. Jesus has shown me the truth. I too asked Him to pardon me, Willem. I will help Tiberius when you leave."

"Does the beautiful woman live here in the palace?"

"Yes. She will be glad for me, and I will tell her about Tiberius." He paused and said, "You better whistle before you go inside. They can hear you better out here."

I whistled, and they answered.

I thanked Plenius, and he stepped up and surprised me with a hug.

Pater whistled later when he returned from seeing Tiberius the second time, and Mater and I answered. I was really curious about what they discussed.

Soon Plenius brought me food, so I ate and rested. We remembered to whistle every now and then as the long day wore on. We had an evening meal, then Plenius said, "Sleep here tonight, and wear your own clothes early tomorrow, for you will be returning to Rome."

Before I lay down to rest, I whistled one last time, and heard their answers. Then I knelt down by my cot. I really had some thanking to send up that night. *Jesus, you have been so good to me. You saved my emperor! You saved Plenius! You saved us! Thank you, Jesus; thank you, Father; and thank you, Holy Ghost!*

The next morning I was awakened by Pater's "Tawheet!" I rose up and dressed in a hurry. Plenius brought me a tray of food—good-tasting fish, with some toasted bread and cheese, some ripe olives, and a mug of sweet juice. I ate every bit of it and finished the last drop of the juice.

Soon Plenius knocked on my door and came in. "Your escort will come for you soon. Thank you, Willem, for praying for me. I know you did. I don't know what will happen to me when Tiberius dies, but if I ever get free, I will try to find you."

"Thank you for your kindness, Plenius. Somehow, I believe you will be freed."

When the soldiers came they brought Mater and Pater with them. We headed back along the winding trail to the outpost. Coming down the cliff we were treated to the glorious view of the blue water and fluffy white clouds floating in the early sky. The air was cool, but the sun was doing much to warm the day.

At the outpost, we stood around a fire until a boat drew up to the beach. The two sailors told us and our soldier escort to get in so they could row us to the ship anchored out in the deeper water. The fresh air felt good on my face as the sailors rowed us out to the ship. Mater smiled at me.

"I hope you won't get sick this time," I said.

The ship took us in and began the journey north to Rome. As the ship sailed away from Capri, I sighed out loud. "What a trip!"

Pater laughed. We three sat snuggled up on an outside bench against the cabin of the ship. Mater was looking weak like she did when we came over. I got up and said, "Mater, lie down now, and maybe you won't be as sick as before."

She laid her head on Pater's lap, and he covered her over with the soft gray blanket that had served us all so well on the trip. In a few moments she seemed to fall asleep.

"I hope she sleeps the whole way," Pater said quietly.

I leaned on the rail, and said in a low voice, "Pater, may I ask you what you and the emperor talked about?"

"The first time he wanted to know about our church. I was surprised at his interest. He told me he knew my record, and was astounded that one of his legionnaires would find such work agreeable after living the soldier's life. His voice was gruff, but he didn't seem angry that we had the church.

"I told him the Lord chose me to be the pastor of the children, and that it was as challenging as the life I lived in his army. Then he turned and asked Mater about you—how long had you been a worshipper of Jesus, had you ever worshipped the Roman gods, and were you an honest boy? Mater told him the truth, and he grunted his thanks."

"The Lord knew he meant us no harm, didn't He, Pater?"

"He did. The emperor seemed to be trying to verify if we were true believers in Jesus, especially you, son. I saw him as a very sick man, who was trying to hold up against collapse. There was another man with him at our first meeting. Was he in there when you went?"

"No, sir. We two were alone."

"This man seemed to be a counselor to him. Perhaps he was the astrologer named Thrasyllus who I'd heard had been at Tiberius' right hand for quite awhile. I heard him say before Tiberius questioned us, 'The message, sire, was very plain. The stars spoke of a boy leading you out. I cannot tell if this is the one.'"

I told Pater all that happened with Plenius and Tiberius. Then I asked, "Did the emperor tell you that Jesus saved him?"

"Yes, that's why he wanted to see me again. He asked me for advice."

"He did?" Mater exclaimed. We were both surprised when she spoke. "I'm all right if I just lie still. But I want to hear all about what happened, so I haven't been asleep. Lucius, you gave the emperor your advice?"

"Yes, I did."

"What advice, Pater?"

"He wanted to know what he should do about all the false gods in Rome. He wanted to do whatever he could to correct the wrong beliefs the people had been taught."

Mater asked, "What did you tell him?"

"I told him to sponsor Jesus, and not attempt to tear down the others. There wasn't enough time for him to see to it being done."

"Did he agree, Lucius?"

"Yes. He seemed relieved about it. He said he would issue a request immediately to the Senate for Jesus Christ to be placed among the approved gods of the Romans."

"That is amazing, Pater. Do you think they'll do it?"

"Perhaps if he lives long enough to push for it."

266

"Do you think he will live much longer?"

"It's in the Lord's hands, son. As long as he is alive, he needs us to pray for him."

So we did just that. As we prayed, the Holy Ghost took over, and it seemed the Holy Ghost prayed for Tiberius, and for all of Rome, and then for all the lands and people the Roman roads led to.

As the ship sailed on, Mater lay covered up on Pater's lap, and I leaned over the rail thinking about going back to Rome. It was still a dirty, wicked city. I had thought I wanted to leave it more than anything else in life. But the work I had been doing, preaching in the Forum, and now my meeting our emperor and seeing him saved, had somehow changed my mind.

In just a few hours I would be back there with my fraters and Elise, the church, and Rabbi Saul and Simeon. I wanted to see Nicholas' face when we came back safe from Capri. And I wanted to preach to the thousands of lost Romans there so Jesus could save them and the Holy Ghost could fill them. And I wanted to see Blue's believing face among them!

Looking out over the deep Great Sea, I found myself dreaming of the city I knew so well. I was glad I was headed back to Big Ugly, the wicked and wonderful city of Rome, my home. *Thank you, Jesus!*

A.D. 56

.

EPILOGUE

"IT'S an open letter from Jerusalem, Willem."

I was busy trying out a new song on my harp. "Can you tell who it's from?"

"The letter begins, Paul, called to be an apostle, separated unto the gospel of God…"

She's teasing me again!

"Elise! Stop!" I stood up and laid my harp aside. "You're just saying that! You know how excited I am to meet that great man Lanee wrote us about."

"All right, Willem— Rome's great preacher—*you* read it. You'll see that I'm telling you the truth."

I questioned her warm brown eyes as I took the much-handled parchment. What I saw was a large ornate *Paul* at the head of the letter.

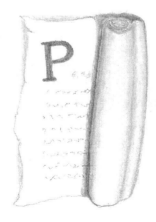

"It *is* from him!" I sent her a look of apology, then hungrily read, "'to all that be in Rome, beloved of God, called to be

271

saints: Grace to you and peace from God our Father, and the Lord Jesus Christ.' And listen to this, Elise!—'First, I thank my God through Jesus Christ for you all, that your faith is spoken of throughout the whole world.'"

I sat back down to soak up the words. I thought of the thousands of times I'd preached in Rome. *Of you, my Lord Jesus!*

Elise flashed her smile at me. "...spoken of throughout the whole world..." she repeated. "Remember how it started with all of us children, Willem?"

I answered my perfectus wife, "Yes, I remember."

Then I let my heart fly upward for a moment. *I remember it all started when you showed a girl in Palestine that you loved me.*

FACT OR FICTION IN WILLEM'S GOD

WILLEM'S God is a work of fiction with much truth interspersed. So what is fiction and what is fact?

How soon after Jesus Christ lived and died did Christianity come to Rome? As early as A.D. 64 Christians were persecuted in Rome. So sometime between A.D. 33 and that date, someone brought the gospel to the Imperial City.

Did children really start the church in Rome? No one knows, but God. I have imagined that Lanee's witness to the children was the beginning. What do you think?

Did concrete exist in Rome? "The ancient Romans developed cement and concrete similar to the kinds used today." says the World Book Encyclopedia. The article gave this surprising information: "People lost the art of making cement after the fall of the Roman Empire in the A.D. 400's." Not until the 18th century did a British engineer named John Smeaton again find how to make it.

Did people have "honeymoons" back then? I don't know. The wedding trip the four young people took to Rome may have been just a gift, and not part of a "honeymoon" tradition.

Did Tiberius Caesar ever go back to Rome? I wrote in Willem's God that he was on his way back when Willem and Mater saw him on the barge. He actually did this, but, according to history, at sometime during the trip he discovered his pet snake had been killed and was being eaten by hundreds of ants. Perhaps because he was superstitious, he turned around and went back to Capri. (Did he imagine hundreds of Romans swarming over his dead body?) For whatever reason, he never set foot in Rome again.

Did Tiberius believe in Jesus, and did he get saved? It is a matter of record that Tiberius, before he died, petitioned the Senate to allow Jesus Christ to be honored among the approved gods of the Romans. It is not known whether he was saved or not. I chose to write that he was. If Jesus had influenced him enough to know He should be worshiped, then He could have influenced him enough to be saved.